TITLE PAGE

THE GHOSTS OF MORLEY MANOR

W. J. Cooper Copyright 2019

All Rights Reserved

Sketches by C.L. Vanchina

TO DAN   W Cooper

AUTHOR'S NOTES

Many of us have had brushes with the unexplainable. The unknown that while seeming far-fetched to those who do not believe it does not make them any less real. Any less true. It happened. We were there.

This book was based on two true events. That I stand on. I need no one's permission as they were part of me. I took those two truths and developed them into a story. The following are the truths. The remainder is a creation for the reader's interest and entertainment.

"For those who believe, no proof is necessary. For those who don't believe, no proof is possible."

- Stewart Chase -

THE ATTIC

Where It Began

Growing up I would visit my grandparent's home. Grandma always had a big bed for kids at the bottom of the stairs. Kids just were not allowed to sleep up there. We were not allowed to venture upstairs unless given express permission which I doubt that ever happened. My grandmother would say there is no reason for us to be up there or nosing around in the attic where she kept her things. It wasn't questioned. It is just the way it was. So it was no big surprise that when my mother purchased it in the late seventies the attic is the first place I wanted to wander through.

When I unlatched the hook and walked in (The attic was on the same level as the bedroom partitioned off with the door.) I was met with disappointment. I thought surely I would find some clandestine reason for it having been off limits. It's most frightening attributes were the spiders who had claimed tenancy. It was just...an attic.

Over the years that followed I had been in and out of there umpteen times as it was storage space. Some days I would recall that first visit and smile. How gullible I had been. I actually believed there was a story in that attic. However, in 1990 my oldest daughter, who was named for my grandmother experienced chilling encounters there that would forever alter my ability to smile or laugh at that room ever again. Almost thirty years later. We still stand on every word.

GEORGE

Her Story

This is my story. I remember every detail as if it all just happened yesterday. One day I came into the house after playing with my sister and the neighborhood kids, upset that all of them were being mean to me. I decided that I didn't want to play with them anymore and that I was going to make up an imaginary friend to play with instead. I turned on the radio and began singing along with the song that was already playing on the country station, "Ghost In This House" by Shenandoah. I wondered what my newly created friend's name should be. Then I heard a voice in my head say the name "George." Being the first name that popped in my head, it seemed suitable. George was now my imaginary friend.

Or so I thought. Within the next few weeks, George went from being someone who I knew was imaginary when I created him, into a real person. For some reason George only wanted to play in the attic. It was a convenient play place because the attic was directly next to our bedroom. By this time, there was no rule or razor straps forbidding any children to set foot in there. My mom thought nothing of my mentions of George or me playing in the attic at first. It wasn't until a few weeks later when she noticed something wasn't right, but in fact, seriously wrong. I do not remember much past being in the attic that day, except the part of my mother slapping me across the face and dragging me out of there. At dinner she'd told me what happened. Apparently when I didn't respond to her calling me, she came into the attic to investigate. She found me sitting on the floor, playing with a creepy old doll, talking to myself. After the third time of her trying to get my attention, she yelled my name. "Are you listening to me? Get up and come downstairs." I whipped my head around. My eyes rolled in the back of my head and in a voice that was not from a nine year old girl but that of a grown man's I screamed "NO!" It scared her so much that she slapped me across the face, pulled me up off the floor to snap me out of it and dragged me out of there. After telling me what happened she said I was not allowed under ANY circumstances to ever go into the attic again. The next night I started talking in my sleep.

A couple weeks before George came into my life I found a picture of my dad and I sleeping when I was a baby. I asked my grandma if I could have this picture. Of course she agreed. I slept with that picture under my pillow every night since the day my grandma gave it to me. The day after my mom forbid me to go into the attic again I made my bed and put the picture back under the pillow as usual. My family went to hang out at my aunt's house and when we got home it was time for bed. I got into my pajamas and snuggled underneath my blankets. Since I can remember to this day I sleep on my stomach with my hands above my head underneath my pillow. I positioned myself to where I was comfy and immediately noticed the picture wasn't where I had placed it earlier. It wasn't there at all. That night George came to me in my dream and asked me why I had not come in to play with him that day. My mom noticed I was talking in my sleep when in reality I was explaining myself in my sleep.

For the next week I searched high and low for the missing picture of my father and me. And every day I heard George's voice telling me to come to the attic. I kept telling him I wasn't allowed. He was getting more frustrated with me every time I told him no. Each night as I slept he would show up in my dreams and we would argue. He would tell me to come and I would repeat myself telling him I wasn't allowed. Throughout the weeks our arguments became more heated. I was no longer talking in my sleep but yelling even screaming sometimes. That last night that George visited my dreams was the last time I ever saw or heard from him again. He came to me and held up the missing picture that I had searched everywhere for. He actually said to me, "Haven't you been looking for something?"

I said, "Give me back my picture." as I reached for it. He held it up high so I was jumping up and down trying to get it back from him. He laughed at me as he taunted me with it and told me to come to the attic and in return he would give me back the photograph I so badly wanted. I started screaming as I fought him not only in my dream but in reality as well. Imagine a child trying to physically fight off the likes that horror films are made of while they sleep. That is how it was.

My mom who was on the other side of the wall in her room heard me screaming at the top of my lungs and flailing again. She was afraid to wake me it was so bad that she feared I would be traumatized if she did. Then she heard me shout, "GO BACK TO WHERE YOU CAME FROM. I NEVER WANT TO SEE YOU AGAIN." He looked at me, laughed and said, "You will regret this." I was only nine. I didn't know what regret meant but to me it was a threat. Suddenly I felt a vibration coming from the attic towards the bunk beds where my sister and I sleep. I started screaming and repeating "NOOOOOOO," because I knew he was going to do something. I couldn't open my eyes. I felt as if I had no control over what was going to happen. I could no longer scream. I felt like I couldn't breathe. Everything was silent but I could still feel George's presence in the room.

Just then the alarm went off and all that was heard was a loud KABOOM! We opened our eyes as my mom bolted into the room and turned on the light. I saw the missing picture laying on the floor next to my little sister as she lay face flat on the wooden floor with her hands covering her nose. My mom told her not to move her hands and raced for a towel because there was no doubt by the blood falling between her fingers that her nose was broken if not shattered.

My mom asked my sister who was completely oblivious to what really went on in my might time terrors what had happened. "Did you fall off the top bunk?" "No," she said. "It felt like someone picked me up and then just dropped me." When she got to the doctors he asked her to tell him and her response then was the same as it is twenty nine years later.

  "My sister's imaginary friend broke my nose."

THE VISITOR

Believe What You Want...

In a small Midwest village at the road's end, where the Dead End sign stands between the driveway and the wood's edge sat the last house on the left. (Yes...that is all true) My mother's and my grandparents, before her, home. I made that trip with my teenage daughters in 1993. I was sitting at the big round table in front of the woodstove sifting through some necessary papers. My mother's chair. She was in the intensive care unit fighting for her life. My youngest was still in her coat lounging on the couch since the woodstove hadn't been going that long. We had only been in town a short hour or so after coming from seeing her. The couch butted up to the darkened doorway of my mother's bedroom. She and her sister who was sitting in my grandmother's chair directly in front of me with the wide long wooden armrests were watching television.

I was interrupted from my task by a sudden squabble and the youngest telling the oldest to turn the tv back on. I was so engrossed I did not know it had even went off. I spied the oldest with the remote resting just above her hand on the wood. I sighed heavily. I had no energy for this. "Stop," I admonished her. She says she didn't do it. I told her regardless to turn it back on and leave it alone. Once their attention was back on the program I went back to my work but the calm was short lived as the television went black again. I directed my gaze at her. She, however, was already vehemently denying any involvement.

It was late. I was drained. I felt the best course of action would be to take the remote and I put it in the middle of the table and placed a pizza order. As I hung up the phone no tv. My daughters looked at me and then at the remote in the center of the table. I shrugged and half joking said, "If it happens again we are out of here." The pizza arrived and with more than an hour had passed with no further incidents I stopped wondering about the strange occurrence and finished up. Just as I laid the last piece of paper onto the table there was a sudden invisible, soundless movement in her room. It's hard to describe. You couldn't see or hear it but...you felt it. Bone chilling felt it. My eyes were riveted on my youngest who was already in motion as an icy trail of air coming from her room passed between us. I screamed for her sister to get her coat but my youngest was way ahead of me already grabbing it and pushing her out the door. Just as we reached the exit the tv which sat in the corner next to it went black for the fourth time. I turned the lock and slammed the door behind us not wanting them in there one more minute.

We stayed the night at a neighbor's house. At daybreak I said we would go back and get their stuff. They weren't so keen on that but I convinced them with false bravado (No one had forgotten) that whatever had happened the night before was long gone with the daylight. Since there was no front door key we crept in from the back and used that entrance. As we did so it as with caution. My youngest was so close behind me I could feel her pressing up against me and had her sister in tow. She questioned me again if I was sure it was a good idea. I assured her it would be okay. As I turned the key and pushed open the door my breath caught in my throat. I was stopped by the chain lock. My heart was beating wildly in panic as she whispered, "Mom, you didn't..." "I know," I replied. I have a fear of chain locks. I NEVER use them. A direct result of too many horror movies where they would have made it but for that.

I backed away and started to say, "Get in the car." But there was no need. The oldest was already at the driveway with her sister right behind her. I'm not even sure if I shut the slightly ajar door nor did I care. The ride home was different than any other long road trip we have been on together. Quiet. No teens bickering. No teens talking a million miles a minute. We each were lost and in shock in our own thoughts. The television. The chain lock. I couldn't get over it all the way home and beyond what we had experienced. Something had not wanted us there. We were the visitors and it was us who were not welcome there. We will never forget. We will never be able to let anyone try to explain it away. It will never be possible for us. You cannot explain away the truth with a coincidence.

We, alone, were the ones who were there.

Dedicated to Sarah & Jenny

PROLOGUE

Allison McDonald had no idea what awaited her as she stepped out of her old car to survey the property she had inherited. It seemed her great uncle, Sebastian Morley, had bequeathed it to her as his only living relative much to her surprise. She had heard of him once or twice but she had never, in fact, even met him nor spent a single day in the house that was now going to be her home. What an eyesore she thought! It was sure to take up all the monies that had been included to bring this place up to code. Nestled about two hundred yards from the railroad tracks which by the looks of them they had not been used in decades at the road's end completely surrounded by woods sat Morley Manor.

CHAPTER ONE

Morley Manor

As she walked up the cobblestone path that led to the massive double oak doors she wished she had taken the lawyer up on his offer of viewing the house and ten acres with her. It was foreboding even in the bright sunlight that filtered through the trees. She looked around her wondering what it was going to be like at night for her alone in the woods. She shivered despite the eighty degree day. She spotted an old barn that had seen its better days and cringed. How much was that monstrosity going to cost to fix up? The roof was in bad need of repair as well as the sagging sliding doors. Mr. Bane had told her that her that Sebastian Morley had been a recluse up until the time he entered a nursing facility and that the place had sat empty for over five years. He had rented the property out for ten years prior to that but no tenants had stayed long. He was uncomfortable when she asked him why that was exactly. He only replied that it had been for different reasons. She was suddenly grateful that ten thousand dollars had also gone with it. It would take at least that much if the interior resembled the outside at all. The exterior had good bones being made of stone but the windows that she could see from the front were all broken. She ticked off the cost to replace them. Ugh. How many more would she find? The roof, like the barn, was in need of replacement as well.

She reached the entrance and fished in her bag for the key. "Don't be such a fraidy cat," she admonished herself. "Its old that's all." Even with her small pep talk she pushed the doors open with trembling fingers and walked in. She stood in the middle of the great room which boasted a cavernous wall to wall fireplace also made of stone and cathedral ceiling with beams. She spied a mouse running across the floor to her left. Of course, she thought, making a mental note to contact a pest control company. Beyond the great room sat a kitchen that while large needed a lot of work in updating and a new floor to boot. The appliances, however, seemed to have survived. There was a mud room in the back of the kitchen with doors that led out to the side and a bath with a claw foot tub. She would get to that later after inspecting the rest of the two story house. Off the great room was a sitting room and one huge bedroom. Yikes! The windows in there were also broken. It smelled musty but that was a given seeing no one had lived there for a long time. The wood floors were coated in dirt and would need to be re- sanded and stained but that was a project she may be able to take on herself. In the sitting room were the stairs to the second level. Why did she feel dread in having to go up them. Stop being paranoid she told herself and just do it. There was a wall lamp at the landing which reminded her that there were no utilities yet and she would have to finish up here soon and locate a hotel in the area until she could have them turned on.

At the top of the stairs was a fair sized room that was just there. No rhyme or reason, no door with slanted walls that she guessed were plaster. Another cost! There was a door that separated it from the other room and off of that the attic. She had never seen an attic on the same level of a home. They, in her experience, were above and had drop down ladders to gain access. She unhooked the makeshift lock and went in. It was creepy. Dust particles were circulating in the rays of light that came through its one window. There were cobwebs everywhere. Great...one had a nasty looking spider in it. She would have them spray for those too. She hooked the door and went back downstairs. It was almost six. She needed to get dinner. She hadn't ate since breakfast wanting to get on the road for the four hour drive from her apartment in the city. She had driven past Main Street on her way through. Surely there were would be somewhere to eat down that road. The property would have to wait until tomorrow. In the daytime she said firmly as she locked the door.

Main Street was off the highway and was in reality just two short blocks long before it gave way to a residential area. She parallel parked in front of a worn sign that read Josie's Fine Food. It sat next to the hardware store which in turn sat next to the post office. On the other side of the street was a beauty salon an antique shop which she would visit soon and a library. Further down were eight or ten more buildings that she could not see signs for. They must be on the storefronts themselves she surmised. Small town living. What a change this would be from the hustle and bustle of the big city.

A heavy set lady with an open friendly face greeted her with a smile and told her to take a seat anywhere. She and two others, old men sitting at the counter drinking coffee, were the only ones there. It was a homey atmosphere with its checked tablecloths and the pictures of what was probably the town in days gone by on the walls. She came over and handed her a menu her curiosity immediately piqued. She knew everyone but she did not recognize this slip of a girl whom she judged to be in her late twenties. They did get an occasional stranger passing through but not often. She wiped her hands on her apron. By the end of dinner she would glean as much information out of her as possible. She still had two hours before closing. Why not make good use of her time?

"What can I get for you honey," she asked as Allison put her menu back in its holder. "What is the special." she asked already eyeing the banana cream pie in the glass case on the side wall. "Well, not to sound like I am bragging but we have a Club Sandwich on Rye that will knock your socks off." Allison smiled at her. "Then I will take that and a cup of coffee." While she waited for her order she got out a piece of paper and ink pen and began writing a list of things that needed to be done, Perhaps, she thought, her waitress may be able to recommend a reliable, good handyman. Certainly there had to be one around. She also made a list of items she would need. Cleaning supplies, a few groceries but that would have to wait until the electric was on. A flashlight and batteries for emergencies. A couple of candles would not be a bad idea either.

When the woman brought her coffee she asked if there were accommodations nearby. "Are you staying long," she inquired before answering. Allison sighed. "I actually just moved here from downstate. I am going to be fixing up the old Morley Manor but it's not suitable for habitation yet. Morley Manor? Good grief! She had her work cut out for her! Not to mention the other things. She went back up to the front and brought her a business card and the name of a local motel a few miles away. She apologized that there were no hotels. "It's not much to look at but it is clean and you will be quite comfortable there." Allison thanked her and accepted the card she held out to her. Jake Madden – Construction. Honest, Reliable. Free Estimates. She told her as she read it that if she was fixing up the old house and did not already have a contractor that he was the best. Allison confided that she did not.

"You may think I am biased. Jake is my nephew. I raised him since he was a toddler but he really is the finest man for the job."

She took that in. A contractor that offered free estimates? Just what she needed. "Thank you," she said. "This is a big help. That would have been my next question." The woman smiled at her again and went to get her food. When she returned she placed it in front of her and sat down. "My name is Josie." "Oh, as in the owner?" "Yep. The one and only!" "Hello Josie, My name is Allison McDonald but you can call me Ally." Josie considered her patron. She was pretty with big brown eyes. Doe eyes is what they used to call them. Her hair was in a bun but she was certain it would fall to her waist if she wore it down. She seemed nice, polite even. A lot of people who stopped in that were not from these parts looked down at her establishment like they were too good for it. This girl, she was also certain of, was different. "I hope you do not mind that I joined you but we don't stand much on ceremony around here." "No, not at all," she replied. "I'm glad for the company." She was nice. Ally liked her right off. Josie went to refill her cup and brought her own drink back to the table and sat down again. "Whew," she exclaimed, "the old Morley place! How in the world did you come by that? I heard Sabastian passed recently. Did you purchase his estate?"

"Did you know him? He was my great uncle." Josie filed that away. "Everyone who is past the age of sixty knew of him." "Oh. I never met him myself. He left it to me when he died." "I've never seen the place before today." Josie filed that too. Ally was going to be in for a heck of a surprise in taking it on. She thought of all the rumors that had spread throughout the years about it. Something was not quite right there. The kids labeled it a haunted house and if she had to go by the stories that former tenants had regaled her with she was concerned that she would be out there all alone. As she ate Josie considered whether she should bring it up but decided against it. If there were any truths to the gossip she would find out soon enough on her own. When Ally was finished she thanked Josie again for the recommendation of her nephew. "You were right," she added, "the sandwich was terrific." Josie smiled at her. She told her it was best if she contacted Jake tonight so he could possibly meet her there tomorrow. "Or better yet, how about right now," she said as he walked in the door. Ally looked up to see a man of about forty coming towards them. He had dark hair that was cut short almost in a crew cut and blue piercing eyes with rugged handsome features. She guessed him to be about six foot two. As he came up he put his arms around Josie. "How is my favorite girl?"

She beamed at him. Her pride and joy. "We were just talking about you." "How so," he asked noticing Ally. Who was she? She was a looker. Definitely not anyone he knew. Josie made the introductions explaining her situation. "Morley Manor huh?" Ally grimaced inside. Why did it seem like he, too, had reservations about her new home? It was not her imagination. "I have a few things going right now but I can come by in the morning if you would like and take a look see. To be truthful I've always wanted to see inside of it." It was decided that they would meet here at the restaurant around nine am. "If you have not had the pleasure of my aunt's breakfast then you are in for a real treat," he told her. Ally did not doubt that. The banana cream pie was still calling her name. She ordered it. Josie cut her a huge slice. She needed to gain some weight she thought. Jake watched her as he took a seat at the counter. She was all of five foot two with a slight figure. Very nice he thought but the manor?

What an undertaking. He hoped she would be up to the task. Even though he had not been inside the grounds were in need of some care and that old barn. Ugh. Was it even worth saving? He had passed by there several times and on one occasion stopped to look at it but did not want the cost of fixing it for himself. That, along with all the weird stuff that happened there was enough for him to shelve any ideas of taking it on. He did not believe in hauntings or the paranormal but there were a lot of things that could not be explained. If you believed the rumors and gossip surrounding it he added to himself.

She took her time with the pie. It was heavenly and obviously homemade. No way could you get this in a store. Her eyes kept glancing over to where Jake sat. His powerful frame filled the stool. He seemed okay. The free estimates were his biggest attraction. Besides his terrific smile and good looks she said smiling to herself. It was at that moment that he turned around. What was she smiling about? Their eyes met. Oh great, he saw me. He thinks I'm smiling at him. He nodded to her as he got up to leave. Morning was going to be one he would be looking forward to.

CHAPTER TWO

New Friendships

At exactly nine am Ally walked into the restaurant. Jake was already there. He gave her a big smile when he saw her. They took a table and he ordered the special which was eggs, bacon and potatoes for both of them. As an afterthought he told Josie they would split an order of biscuits and gravy as well. "You cannot leave here without having them. They are a necessary staple," he told her. "Worth every penny but I am buying." She shook her head saying that he did not have to do that but Jake was not taking no for an answer. Any new person in town, especially this woman was nothing to pass up a chance to get to know. He excused himself for a moment and returned with the coffee pot and two cups.

He poured for them telling her that his aunt was short a waitress today so after checking out the manor he was going to be coming back to lend a hand. Ally regarded him. He did not seem domesticated to her. His chiseled jaw, his dark tanned skin, his huge biceps that his white t-shirt did little to hide, nothing about him said kitchen help. He smiled. He knew what she was thinking. "It's just me and my aunt. I do whatever I can." She took that in. How nice it must be to have family. Her own parents had passed on years ago in a car accident when she was eighteen. She missed them.

When their food arrived He gave Josie a wink. She kissed him on the cheek. He was a good boy. He gave up his own time to fill in for her often. Ally watched the exchange. She felt completely at ease with these two people that she had only met last night. She was suddenly glad she had stopped in. Over breakfast Jake asked questions. What were her goals? Would she live there or resell it? "No, I won't be selling," she replied. "I intend to make it my home once it is finished." He asked about her lodgings. He said he hoped it was suitable. Why did he care? A room was a room. She assured him it would serve the purpose until she could move in. "I need to call the power companies. Once they are turned on I plan on staying there." Interesting. He found himself wondering if she was going to be afraid to be in that rambling old place all by her lonesome. Again, why did he care? She was an ends to a means. A client.

When breakfast was over she had to admit he had been correct about the biscuits and gravy. He suggested she ride with him and afterwards he would bring her back. Ally was about to decline but it would give her the opportunity to go to the hardware and then asked him about the grocery store which he said was about a mile out of town on Route Four. He opened the truck door for her and got behind the wheel. Why had he asked her to ride with him? He wondered if he had gone all soft. He liked having her there beside him though even if he was not sure quite why just yet.

"Wow! Impressive," he said once they closed the doors. The fireplace would need a bit of attention as some of the stones were loosening but that was an easy task. He admired the craftsmanship of the carved woodwork and the rich mahogany walls of the great room. He was going to take the job if just to put them back to their original splendor. He glanced back over at the fireplace again picturing a fire blazing brightly in it on a cold winter evening. The Midwest winters could be brutal. His next thought was the two of them together sitting on the floor in front of it. What the hell was going on? Did he need to remind himself that he was here to work not to engage in romantic notions with a woman he did not even know? Any woman for that matter. It had been years since he had been with one. He did not miss it either. "Is something wrong," Ally asked as she saw his features harden. Had he changed his mind so soon? Was it too much for him? He had not even seen the rest of the rooms. "Huh?" He pushed his thoughts away. "Sorry, was thinking."

They went to all the rooms and he inspected each thoroughly. Yes the floor would have to be replaced in the kitchen. He would take it down to the subfloor but he advised her that it, like the ceiling, probably had more than one layer, possibly more than two. Old houses were like that. The mud room had a washer and dryer connections that was a bonus but it would need a laundry tub to drain into. He also said he would like to have the electric as well as the two twenty outlet looked at. He was certain some of it would need to be rewired just going by the age of the house. The bathroom would require new tiles as many of them were missing or broken. It did not appear many updates had been made to its original state. With every new sentence Ally calculated possible money damages. Ten grand would not go far if he was indeed right about that. She could of course add her savings to it. She had hoped to hang on to them until she could secure work but she would have to do whatever it took to finish what she started.

Upstairs he told her that the plaster should probably come down and drywall put up but if she was not going to be using that part of the house it could wait. There was some work here but it was mostly cosmetic besides the kitchen which he would see to first. He told her that. "So you will take the job?" "Yes Ally. I will." The casual use of her first name surprised both of them. "I actually am excited to get started. This place is amazing." "A contractor's dream." It was settled then. She was glad to have that behind her and glad that he would be the one working on it. Why she did not know but she liked him.

"It will take me a month or so to get it done but I'm up for it." She considered that. "How long before I could move in?" "I mean I do not want to pay for a motel for that long." He got it. That was an expense that would add up quickly. "If you do not mind me being underfoot you could move in as soon as you get the utilities on." That brought him to a question he wanted to ask her since last night. "Are you sure you will be okay here by yourself? At night? It's a bit secluded." She assured him

that she would hoping her bravado hid her inner
fears. She was going to have to make the best
of it and eventually she would get used to it.
They went out to look at the barn. Despite the
roof and doors it was in surprisingly good
shape inside. He felt it would be of use to
her and that she should think about keeping it.
If she ever did decide to sell it would add to
the price. "You wouldn't have to start on it
now. It could wait until spring." Ally looked
at him. He was very competent she was sure.
She would listen to any of his ideas or plans
and most likely approve of them.

Over lunch which Jake insisted on paying for
again they made plans to start on Monday. The
lights and hot water would be on by noon. When
Ally told him he could not continue to pay for
her meals he just laughed. "I will be getting
enough of your money." When she finished her
salad and Iced tea he walked her out before he
had to cover Josie's absent employee. Ally
went to the hardware store. It had all she
needed and more. For a small town it was a
large building and incredibly well stocked. As
she shopped she was aware that the man behind
the counter was watching her in the round
mirrors situated so that they gave him a
vantage point to keep an eye out for possible
shoplifters as she went down the aisles. She

put him at close to sixty with a receding hair line and glasses. She assumed, he too, knew everyone and was wondering who his new customer was. She did not have to wait long. As he rang her up he informed her that his name was Mitchell Hamilton and this was his shop. "So you are staying at the manor eh?" How could he know that? When her saw her confusion he went on to say, "My brother Sid was at Josie's yesterday." "Word travels fast." He gave her a toothy grin. "Yep, sure does. I hear you hired Jake Madden. Good choice!" "Yes, he seems to know his trade. I have every confidence in him."

Hamilton paused. He seemed to be on the verge of telling her something but gave her the total instead. When she had paid for her purchases he walked her to the door and opened it for her. Ally thanked him and said it was a pleasure to make his acquaintance. He replied, "Likewise." Then in a strange voice he added, "you be careful out there miss." She saw the change in his expression. It was no longer cheery but serious now. Concerned even. It rattled her for a second. Stop, she chided herself. He was merely making reference to the manor's seclusion. "Please call me Ally and thank you. I will." "Alright then, Ally, if you need any assistance let me know and I will help or refer you to someone who can." That was very nice of him she thought stowing her bags in the trunk.

Her next stop was the post office. She asked the moody looking elderly lady for a change of address form. When she had filled it out she took it back up to the counter where she was told she would be assigned a box and a number and any mail she received could be collected after eight am. Ally handed her the paper when she heard a distinct gasp even though the woman tried to cover it up. She could not believe her eyes. Another family was going to try to habitate the manor? Good luck with that she thought. "Welcome to Edgerton," she said warily. "We are happy to have you and your family." Ally told her it was just her but she was certain she would like small town living once she got used to it. She cleared her throat as she considered the young woman. She told her that her name was Clara Finley and that her husband Ed was the postmaster. "We knew the former owner. He was crazy as an outhouse rat on meds." Ally did not reveal her relation to him but waited for her to continue.

"I'm sure you have already been filled in on the other stuff." "What other stuff?" Clara shifted her weight, dodging the question and quickly changed the subject. Just last week Ed had scolded her for gossiping. He said it did not look good. "There is bingo on Wednesday nights up to the Veteran's Hall and Leasons's Grocery sale paper comes out twice a month on Fridays. Ally knew she was being put off. She looked at the woman for a long moment. She could not force her to say what was so obviously on her mind. She sighed inwardly. "Thank you," she said and was given her box and two keys. As she walked out she heard whispering. Clara Finley was already talking to the lady next to her. Ally was certain she was the topic.

Friday, armed with garbage bags she set about clearing the main yard of its trash. She would have to find a landscaper to do the lawn. Mr. Bane had it done a few weeks before she arrived but apparently they had not seen fit to do more than maneuver around the litter that was scattered around. She braved the tool shed out by the barn and found an old wooden chair which she dragged in and used to clean the dozens of prisms of the chandelier in the great room as well as all of the globes downstairs. The upstairs would have to wait. She tried but every time she reached the landing she broke out in a cold sweat and turned back. Wonderful. How was she going to live there if she would not brave those steps? She was sure the sensation would pass but she was not going back up until it did. Saturday she found herself at the hardware again. Her eyes went to Josie's but Jake's truck was nowhere to be seen. He does have a job she told herself. You are not his only source of income.

"Hello Mr. Hamilton," she said in greeting. He corrected her with another toothy grin which she found to be quite endearing. "No. None of that. You call me Mitchell." She smiled. "Okay, Mitchell. Here are the measurements for the windows that need to be replaced. He looked at the lengthy list and told her he happened to have all of the sizes in the back and asked if she would need screens and caulk. Ally had not noticed any screens stored anywhere so she said yes to them. As far as he caulk she had to admit she did not know. She was a Library Resource major and had little if no clue about things like that. Mitchell was nonplussed. He smiled kindly at her as she took out her bank card. "You just tell Jake I have them and he will take care of it." She hesitated a moment. "Can I ask you something?" Mitchell nodded. "When I was here you seemed out of sorts when I mentioned the manor. I got the same from Mrs. Finley at the post office. Why?" "Clara Finley is a busy body. Pay her no mind." "I have a delivery waiting in the back. We will have to talk later...soon." Hmmm. He, too, was dodging her inquiries. She left him then and returned to the motel where she showered and turned in early her muscles aching and sore from her labors.

Sunday morning arrived overcast but warm. She put on a pair of jean shorts and a purple tank. She used a pony tail holder to tie back her hair and headed to Josie's. Skipping dinner had not been a good idea. She was ravenous having only a bag of chips and a soda the previous day. Jake was there when she walked in. "Hey stranger," he said. "Join me." She took a seat as he watched her. She looked nice today. What had she been up to? His aunt had said except for Friday she had not seen her. He was going to stop in at the manor and see if she was there but he could not come up with a plausible excuse. He entertained the idea of inventing one just so he could see her.

Josie came out and sat with them. She was growing to like Ally more every time she came in. It was no secret to her that her nephew already was attracted to her. It rather surprised her. He had not dated since he broke it off with Holly some years ago. That was a union made in hell and she, for one was glad to see it end. Holly was nothing short of a drama queen who found trouble wherever she went and usually it fell back on Jake. She excused herself to ring up three customers. Ally glanced over at her as she called them each by name and made small talk with them as they paid their bill. I like her she thought. She is a good person. When she told Jake the same he agreed she really was.

They shared another order of her famous biscuits and gravy and as they ate she recapped all she had done over the weekend. "Very good," he said. "Are you getting a little more comfortable with being there?" Ally said she was but until the lights were on she would not stay past dusk. Jake chuckled to himself. He doubted she would stay that long. He told her Mitchell called him about the windows and that two of his guys would accompany him in the morning to install them so he could concentrate on the kitchen. Ally noted that he watched her a lot but when their eyes met she held his gaze and did not look away. Josie came back to the table with fresh coffee and after re-filling their cups sat with them again. Jake studied her. What was she thinking? He could tell she had something on that mind of hers. "What is going on," he asked? "Something is bothering you." "How did you know?" He smiled at her. "Your eyes gave you away." She had heard that. Her mother used to tell her the same thing. She did not mean to blurt it out but she said, "I've been getting funny looks and strange comments from people whenever I tell them where I am going to be living. It is like there is a secret and I am the only one who isn't in on it." Three days? A personal best for Edgerton. Josie gave Jake a look that said she needs to know. Jake returned it with an I know one of his own. There was no way past it. Thankfully his aunt took the lead.

"Ally, honey, the manor is said to be haunted by the ghost of a child who died there somewhere around the mid-thirties I think. There have been a lot of unexplained incidents since then. That is why no one has stayed long. They all claim to have been driven out by her. I doubt there is anyone left here that could remember or dispute it. It has become a legend in these parts and like all rumors the story gets bigger each time it is told." "That was nearly a century ago Jake chimed in, "and the only one who could shed some light on it is your uncle and he was a recluse and now he is gone." He could see she clearly was spooked with the things she had just been told. "I don't even know if there is any truth to it to be honest but that is why people have been treating you that way. Most of the old ones believe it and for the younger generations it has become a ghost story of sorts."

He did not take his eyes off of her as she listened. He could tell she was thinking about being out there alone, at night. He saw the fear that she tried to conceal. Great! She had inherited a haunted house? Did she not have enough to worry about? How was she going to live there now? The place was daunting enough in the daylight. Now this? Jake's tone was gentle. "Do you still want to go through with this Ally?" She considered his question for a few moments and replied that she did. "I sold everything I had and gave up my apartment to come here. I am not turning back now." Brave words for a frightened lady. He had to admire her grit. He spoke again, "then do not trouble yourself. If this is something you have to do then Mitchell, Josie and I will be here with you every step of the way." Later when he walked her to her car he said "I am coming to get you in the morning and I will not take no for an answer." This he added in a low tone, "I will take care of you Ally. You can trust in me." They talked a minute longer and then she headed back to the motel. She drifted off with Jake's last words playing in her head.

"I promise, we will figure this out together."

CHAPTER THREE

Emma Morley

Jake knocked on her door at seven am. She answered it and found herself nearly knocked over by the biggest Rottweiler she had ever seen. "Shamus meet Ally. Ally meet your new best friend." "My goodness," she exclaimed startled by his presence. Does he bite?" Jake smiled at her. "He will not bite you but if need be he will take out any threat to you. Other than that he is a one hundred and seventy pound baby." Ally nodded. She held out her hand and was rewarded with a series of slobbery licks. "He likes you already," Jake told her. "I am not good with you being there alone so Shamus here, and I, had a talk last night and we decided that until we get some answers that make sense he will be your new shadow." She wondered if ghosts were afraid of HUGE dogs. She would have laughed at her joke but she wasn't even close to kidding.

When they arrived his crew that consisted of Tim and his brother Mike Moore were already busy with the windows. By noon when the utility guys showed up they were already half done and by quitting time the broken panes would be a memory. Jake concentrated on the kitchen ceiling while the electrical engineer checked out the panel and outlets. Luck was in her favor and they were up to code which surprised all of them. It seems somewhere in the last years there had been a few updates. The hot water tank was also in working order. Another plus. The ceiling upon taking out one of the drop squares was clean to the beams above it. The floor however had two layers and had to be taken to the sub like he had expected. Still, even with that she had saved herself an enormous amount of money. A fact that made her very happy. She would now possibly be able to afford to begin furnishing the house.

By five the windows were all in, the sub floor showing and all the debris hauled away. That was enough for one day Jake conceded. When they locked up they headed to Josie's. Jake gave the dog an affectionate pat as he put him in the fenced yard behind the restaurant. He brought him a dish of food and one for water before he sat down himself. Josie brought them plates. The burgers were juicy and delicious. The fries piping hot and crispy. As they ate

Jake recommended slate tile for the kitchen and told her Mitchell would give them to her at cost. More savings! While Jake went to check on Shamus Josie told her that he was taken with her. She looked at her and said, "No he is not but I do appreciate all he has done and for his concern. He is very sweet." Josie wiped her hands on her apron and laughed. "Yep, sweet on you." When he returned he could tell something had transpired from the look on Ally's face but let it go. If she wanted him to know she would tell him.

"I've been thinking. How would you feel about staying with me tonight? I have an extra room and I promise, your virtue will be quite safe with me." She looked hesitant. "C'mon he coaxed. It will be fine. After all you do have Shamus to protect you." She laughed at that. Yeah, like his dog would protect her from him. To heck with it. She shocked him by saying yes. He gave Josie a huge smile. "See you tomorrow Auntie."

His house sat on five acres and was an A Frame design. Masculine. Exactly what she would have expected. There was a fireplace on the outside wall and the furniture was positioned around it. The home was clean and very comfortable. They talked for a bit and when she yawned he showed her to the room she would be staying in.

"I will take you in the morning to get your car," he said. "Do you need anything? "Pajamas would be nice but I'm sure that isn't going to happen. And a toothbrush." He left the room and came back with one of his shirts that would reach at least to her knees. In his other hand he carried a toothbrush still in its packaging. "The bathroom is to your left. If you want a shower help yourself." When she emerged Jake was sitting in the living room. His bedroom was in the loft above. She thanked him for his hospitality and said goodnight. Long after she was asleep he remained there wondering what it would be like to be with her. Her quiet soft spoken mannerisms, her big brown eyes that held so much. Everything about her drew him in. He felt very protective of her already and would do anything for her which came as a mind numbing thought. No one would get near her or cause her any harm. Not on his watch. He went down the hall before turning off the lights. Shamus lay at the foot of her bed. "Good boy," he whispered. "Take care of her."

While Jake, Tim and Mike manned the sanders Ally took a walk up to the library. She asked if there were any openings for a researcher. She was told by the polite head librarian that there were none at this time but she would have a better chance in Rock Port which was the county seat. She thanked her and then secured a library card and asked to use the computers. After signing in Ally combed the internet for any stories relating to the one Josie had told her. She then asked to be directed to where the microfiche was stored. Once she sat down she searched the thirties but found nothing. She widened her parameters to the late twenties and there it was October Fourteenth Nineteen Hundred and Twenty Nine.

Ten year old Emma Morley, adopted daughter and only child of the late Evelyn and her surviving husband Sebastian Morley found at edge of river adjacent to the family property. Ally was in disbelief. It was true! Emma Morley would have been her second cousin? Third? How horrible. She continued to read what little there was. The death has been ruled an accidental drowning by the county coroner based on the water in her lungs. There will be a private ceremony with the burial to be at an undisclosed location.

How awful. A child had lost her life and the only record of it barely took up a paragraph. She thought of Clara Finley and what she had sad about her uncle. No wonder he was crazy.

His only child had died. She could not even imagine how great his grief must have been. No wonder he was a recluse in that house. He had lived to be one hundred and two years old and had to spend the last eighty two of them without his daughter. She did the math. He had been a kid himself. Barley twenty. She wondered if Emma had been a distant relative or perhaps an orphan and he had taken on that responsibility at such a young age. It saddened her. She searched again for Evelyn Morley finding that she pre dated their adopted child in death by three years from complications in childbirth. At age seventeen he had lost his wife and by twenty his only child. Ally walked back to the manor quite shaken. So sad and yet it did not explain the supposed hauntings and sightings. Were they true or made up tales that had begun with her sudden death? She just did not know.

Shamus met her at the cobblestone walkway and escorted her up the path. When they neared the front door he gave a single deep bark to let his master know his charge had returned. Jake, full of dust from head to foot, met them as they approached the door. Ally was positively pale. "Ally. What is wrong?" She didn't know if it was the strain of the last week or what she had found out but she broke. Silent tears welled up in her eyes and spilled over. Jake led her to a bench in the side yard with Shamus at their heels and sat her down. He put his arm around her and she leaned into him burying her head against his chest and cried. It unsettled him to see her so aggrieved. He would sit with her for as long as took her to recover. He held her until her tears finally subsided shushing her gently and tenderly kissed her forehead. After a time she found her voice and told him all of the details she had learned. In a matter of days she had gone from knowing literally nothing of her uncle to having exposed his grief and loss. Jake understood her sorrow. He understood her fears that still surrounded the house. He understood. He just did not have any answers.

CHAPTER FOUR

Things That Go Bump In the Night

Ally laid out her sleeping bag and threw her pillow on top of it. Shamus watched her intently. She was glad for his company. Between him and having all the downstairs lights burning she felt a bit more at ease. It is amazing what light can do. There were no shadows, there was no fear. She actually was beginning to feel a little silly. Jake called a few minutes before to see if she had changed her mind. "No," she had replied. Her resolve was firmly in place. He told her he would see her early. He had to hand it to her. Scared or not she was standing her ground.

She lie down feeling exhausted but her mind refused to shut down. Shamus lay a few feet from her. He was between her and the open door now. "It's alright boy," she told him softly. "Jake is coming tomorrow." He seemed to understand and put his head on the floor. She used her current insomnia to think about having a portion of the trees removed so she wouldn't feel so cut off from the road. How much would that even be? She would ask Jake. Surely he knew someone with reasonable rates. That in itself would make a big difference. Floodlights would be another good plan. That would be her first step. It meant another trip the hardware but she was beginning to be quite fond of Mitchell so she could use it as a social visit also.

She was still awake at midnight listening to the sounds of the house trying to get accustomed to them. Every home had them. Their own fingerprint in their settling and refrigerator motors. The click and ignition of their hot water tanks. She must have fallen off because when she opened her eyes again it was almost two. She looked at her cell. She thought about calling him but what would she give for a reason? She looked over at the Rottweiler. He had not moved and he was awake as well. It seemed he knew instinctively that she was up. She smiled at him. He was such a good dog. "Go back to sleep" she told him and closed her own eyes once more.

Ten minutes later she heard it. Shamus heard it also. He barked and was at an alert stance in the doorway. Something definitely had hit the floor above her. Chills ran down her spine. Stop it! It was probably a pesky varmint. A raccoon perhaps. That comforting thought lasted all of thirty seconds. Shamus began to back up. Whimpering turned into a sudden fierce growl. The distinct voice of a child calling out to her drawing out each word.

A - L - L - Y. H - E - L - P. M - E.

Ice cold fear washed over her. She was frozen in place. Shamus was now pacing back and forth still growling. His hair standing up along the ridge of his back. She waited but no other sound came to her. Shamus was no longer growling. He went back to whimpering again for a full minute and then he, too, was silent. He did not lay back down, however, he was on his haunches between her and the door again at full alert, his ears perked listening. She grabbed her cell running through her contacts and hit his name. Why had she not put him on speed dial as he suggested?

He picked up before it rang a full time. Was he expecting this? She knew she was babbling but she couldn't get it out fast enough. Jake on the other end trying to make sense of what she was saying. "I didn't imagine it. I was not dreaming. Shamus heard it too." The second she said that he was already on his way out the door. He knew his dog. He did not give out false warnings. It took him less than ten minutes. He had broken every traffic law to do it but he didn't give a damn. Something was very wrong. He let himself in with the spare key that she had given him for the workmen. He would have busted the double doors down if there had not been one. Shamus heard Jake but did not leave Ally's side. He found them both in the bedroom. Ally jumped up and ran to him. Shamus came to him. He patted the dog. "Good Boy Shamus," he crooned as he took Ally in his arms. "Stand down." The dog immediately lay at his feet. "Are you okay," he asked as he held her. "Yes," she replied without a trace of confidence. "It was her Jake. It was Emma."

Jake told her he would be right back and stepped away from her. "Where are you going," she queried, her voice still shaky. "You said you heard a thud upstairs soo..." "I'm going with you." Shamus was on his feet. "Fine but you stay behind us and if something happens, run. Do not stop, do not look back until you get to my truck. The keys are in it and if I am not there by the time you reach it get the hell out of here. Do you understand?" "You are scaring me." He ignored that. His tone was harsh now. "Do you understand," he repeated? Ally nodded that she did. "C'mon boy," he called but it was not necessary the dog was already at his heels waiting.

Jake flipped the landing switch as he ascended grateful that Mike had put new bulbs in earlier that day. He was not afraid of much, anything really, but still he was not itching to be fumbling around in the dark when he need to be able to see what or who may be coming at them. He sent Shamus ahead but the dog did not make any sounds. Jake breathed a small sigh of relief. Had there been even the slightest movement or noise his dog would have reacted. They opened the door to the second bedroom without incident. He pulled the chain on that light also. There was nothing laying around. The floors were bare but the attic door stood wide open. He motioned with a finger to his lips for her to stay quiet and again for Shamus to stay. There was ample light to see inside. The corners were lit by the moon that shone through the window. Nothing. He retraced his steps, fastened the hook and put Ally in the middle of him and Shamus.

When they reached the great room Jake sat her down on the wooden chair. He knelt in front of her so he could see her reaction. "Ally," he said softer now. "I'm sorry if I scared you but I wasn't sure what we would be dealing with." "Which brings to mind," he continued, "remember my words in the future and if we are faced with an unknown, "do NOT make me tell you." "Just do it."

Satisfied that she was listening he also told her that they both needed to get a few hours of shut eye. The Moore's would be there before long. They had a lot to accomplish. He led her into the bedroom turning off the lamps as he went. Ally was eyeing him skeptically. Was that a good idea? When they reached the bedroom she posed that to him. He smiled. "I'm here. Shamus is here and it will be light soon." He unzipped the bag, laid it out like a blanket and told her to lie down. He flicked off the light and in the dark she heard, "Make room." Shamus at their feet, both heads on the pillow, Jake's arm around her they drifted off. No other happenings awakened them. It was not until he heard the pounding on the door that he opened his eyes.

Despite his dis-shelved appearance neither Moore brother commented or gave it a seconds thought. If Jake had stayed, there was a reason. It was not their business to ask why. Tim had his own worries. His wife, Joann had given him grief since taking on this job. She was one of the believers and was worried. To say she was less than thrilled was an understatement. It was all hogwash to him but not her. He let them in and as the dog passed him on his way outside he called to him. "Stay close." The Rottweiler turned back and acknowledged him before trotting off. Jake let Ally sleep until well past eleven. She had quite a fright and wanted her to be refreshed and calmer today.

While Tim went out to retrieve a forgotten tool and she was dressing, he called Mike to the side and in a hushed tone asked if he had been in the attic while changing out the bulbs. Mike shook his head. Jake did not explain. He did not mention anything. Mike's word was enough for him.

"I must have left the door open myself," he said knowing fully well he had not been up there.

CHAPTER FIVE

Ostracized

When she emerged clad in a pair of jeans and black tank Jake motioned for her to follow him. Once out in the yard he told her that he preferred she did not talk about last night to anyone but him. He was speaking in a tone similar to the one he had used then. She did not question him but nodded her assent. If he was telling her to do something she was going to accept it at face value. He whistled and Shamus came running to his side. "Enjoy your stroll did you big guy?" His love for the dog was evident. She admired that about him. They still had not spoken of the occurrence and in an uncanny fashion Jake read her thoughts. "We will sort this out later." She knew he meant once they were alone.

It was half past one. The last floor was sanded. They would take the next three days to apply the coats of varnish and allow an extra day to dry and cure. Mike set about his task of taking down the worn bathroom tiles. Tim, armed with large box traps, was upstairs distributing them just in case there were any coons or possums. In truth Jake could not count that out. He and Alley were in the kitchen. He wore kneepads bent over the last square of tile. He put it in place. The slate had been a good choice. Perfect in fact. She told him so. "I appreciate the offer to stay with you through the drying process," she added, "but that is not necessary. You have done more than enough for me already." A direct reference to his coming to her rescue. "I will get another room."

Jake looked at her as he stood up. "Why does everything have to be a debate with you? Can you not just say okay and accept?" Why was he being so unreasonable? She would be fine at the motel and besides she had her new best friend. Jake addressed her in a very low tone so as to not be overheard. "Look, I do not know what to think. I do not support the ghost theory, but who is really to say they aren't real. One thing I do know is something is amiss here and I would be more comfortable if I can keep you in my sight." "Jake," He cut her off. "This is nonnegotiable Ally. Either you stay where I can keep an eye on you or I'm out." She looked at him incredulously. Was he serious? His blue eyes were hard. Yes. He was serious.

"You would really default on your contract?" He looked her directly in the eye. "Without a second thought." He was not playing. He did not have time or the energy to argue this out. In his mind it was settled. Why did she have to be so solicitous? If he did not want her in his home he would have not made the offer. She drove him to the brink of insanity some days. Her politeness was overwhelming. He did not need her to make life easier for him. He was half tempted to kiss her. How would that suit her gracious sensibilities? He took a step towards her as Shamus ran past him growling. It was just after that they heard Tim's scream of agony. Mike was right behind them. They found him in the attic laying prone, his head against the window sill. His left leg bent at a peculiar angle, his tibia bone protruding. Ally fought off a wave of nausea. A pool of blood was already beginning to form.

Mike reached him first as Jake hit the emergency number on his cell. Within minutes the EMT's arrived. They administered a shot and began an IV of saline. Joann arrived just as they were wheeling him to the awaiting ambulance. Mike had no choice but to call her. His face was ashen, his voice barely above a whisper. "They pushed me." His wife, accompanied by her father began to shout. He was not making any sense. "What are you talking about Tim? Who pushed you?" They all heard his reply. "Both of them." He passed out just after that.

"We will meet you at the hospital," Jake told her his mind whirring with Tim's accusations. Who were "They?" "Thank you she said, "but do not bring her with you!" She addressed Ally next. Her angry voice rising with each sentence. "This is all your fault! You come here stirring up the past. Stirring up the things that hide inside these walls." The driver interrupted before Ally could respond or she say another word. "Ma'am we need to go." Joann's father ushered her to the ambulance doors and helped her up. He was conscious now but incoherent. She was crying as they closed them and took off their sirens wailing. The father took his leave as well. Mike went with him.

Jake, Ally and Shamus stood there for several moments watching as they pulled out onto the highway and took off in the direction of the medical center a few miles away. It was Jake who spoke first. "She didn't mean that. She is just upset. You did nothing wrong." She was not so sure. After last night she knew they were not dealing with the norm. So did Jake. She should have called off the renovations until they could investigate the situation further. What a foolish decision in plunging ahead and now it was Tim, not her, who was paying the price. She did not get what he meant by both of them but Ally was one hundred percent certain that whatever had transpired in the attic and her experience were connected.

"I have to go," he said. Tim had been his friend for years and he had been hurt on his job site. Ally understood. He dropped Shamus off at home and took her to the restaurant. He needed no explanation. Clara Finley had already called and beaten him to it. Joann's mother was her sister. By supper Tim's accident as well as his accusations of being pushed would be a household dinner subject. Ally would be safe with his aunt. He looked at her. She was a wreck. He kissed her lightly on the lips. "I will be back soon." She did not react whatsoever. He wondered if she was in shock. He gave her explicit instructions not to leave and under no circumstances was she to go near the manor and with that he was gone.

The afternoon wore on. She declined food. She couldn't eat. She was sick to her stomach. The picture of Tim's protruding bone, the blood, were lodged in her head. She took a

table in the corner sipping the coffee Josie
had brought aware that the ten or so other
patrons were watching her. She could not
silence his screams nor his last words. The
more she thought about it the more questions it
left her with.

Mitchell came in a few minutes after four
thirty to get a carry out. He sat with Ally
while he waited for it. He already had heard
and had the newest version of the story. What
started out as a fluke accident was now a
deliberate attempt on Tim's life. Leave it to
a small town she thought. That tall tale would
be twice as exaggerated by morning. Mitchell
steered the conversation away from today's
earlier incident. It was bad and he was not
going to make it worse. Worse came anyhow.
Clara Finley walked in just after five when the
post office had closed for the day. With her
was the lady she had seen her talking to on her
trip there.

She made a big to do, loudly, to the other
patrons saying how the newcomer had brought bad
mojo to their town by reviving Morley Manor and
its spirits. There were murmurings amongst the
other patrons. The customers were divided. To
those attentions she had she declared that the
council should call a meeting and ban any
further work until the state police could be

called in. Did she need to remind them that Tim was still in surgery and by his own statement he said he had been pushed? Josie gave her a glaring look and Clara began to speak again but was cut off by Mitchell. "For Pete's sake Clara...shut up! All you do is run your mouth and whatever happened today and any of its consequences are not for you to decide. You are a royal pain in the ass and the only business you do not mind...is your own." Some of them nodded. Some shook their heads in disbelief at Mitchell's outburst but as for Clara she had one more thing to say as she left in a huff. "Mark my words. No good will come from this and we will rue the day we welcomed her to Edgerton."

No one said much after that show. Mitchell took his meal and nodded goodnight to her. He saw Jake who was just pulling up and waited for him to ask about Tim. "He is out of surgery. They had to put in screws and pins to repair the bone. They have him doped up right now but he is going to need a lot of rehabilitation and will be out of commission for some time." Mitchell sighed. He may as well tell him what Clara had tried to start. Jake was livid. Were things not bad enough without her trying to tar and feather Ally? He thanked Mitchell and headed inside. He did not mention that he stopped to make sure the doors were secured and was rewarded by the large great room window having a rock hurled through it with a note that said in bold black letters, go back to where you came from.

As he saw Ally he knew he would not tell her either. He would not add to her misery. He would have it replaced tomorrow. If he could not find anyone to do it after today then he would fix it himself. His head aching with the weight of all that was going on he managed a small smile. He couldn't help but think that this was just the beginning but the beginning of what was something he did not know. Later when Ally was tucked into bed with Shamus standing guard he put in a call to Mike to check for updates. They did not expect any changes in the next few days and he would be home soon. He added that Tim, when questioned had told him that he was welcome to come along but Jake was the only person he would talk to about this. Damn his wife he had said. The less said to her the better.

He made arrangements with Mike to meet around noon. He also told him that work had been cancelled for the next few days if he could even get anyone to go out there. He told him about the broken window. Mike surprised him by saying he would take care of it and then asked him what time he should show up when they started up again? "Thanks," he replied with genuine sincerity, "but why?" "I don't expect you to go back." He laughed a little and then told Jake that the answer was simple, he needed money more than the ghosts did. Jake hung up. That was Mike. Realistic and true blue.

He was laying on the couch nursing his headache when he saw her. He motioned for her to come to him and he moved over to make a space for her to lie down with him. He put his arm around her as she leaned into him and said quietly. "I have to see this through to the end Jake. I have to find out what really is going on there." "I can't leave now, she added in a whisper, "even if I wanted to." Jake held her through the night. He went over her words. He got it. He Ally was determined to solve this mystery and nothing would keep her from it and he would be there beside her when she did.

CHAPTER SIX

Love's Shelter

When she awoke the next morning Shamus was there at her bedside staring at her. She put her arms around him burying her face in his fur. His head rested on her shoulder. He was such a good dog. She was so grateful for his protection. That is how Jake found the two of them. "Someone has a fan," he said lightly. "It goes both ways. I adore him." Jake thought back to Holly. She has not liked him one bit. She would say for him to keep that flea ridden vile creature away from her. She was viler than Shamus ever could be. That brought him a small laugh. Ally looked his way. "What's up?" "Fleas and the difference between truths and outward lies." He laughed again. Ally shrugged. She had no idea what he meant. Whatever it was had nothing to do with what was going on now because this was no laughing matter.

Jake made blueberry pancakes and bacon. He watched her as she ate. "These are great," she told him shoveling another forkful into her mouth. She was positively starving. She had to quit skipping meals. "I learned from the best." He poured fresh coffee. He found himself thinking as he bent over her that even with her hair tied back and in his shirt which was way too large for her that she was beautiful. She wore no makeup. He had not seen her with any since the day they met. That pleased him greatly. He preferred the natural look on a woman.

He was always looking at her or watching her when he thought she wasn't noticing. What was so interesting about her besides her current dilemma? She sighed. He was so kind to stay with her through whatever may happen. She had not wanted to think of how much he had come to mean in such a short time. How much she depended on him. On his strength and his wisdom in the way he looked at things. It hit her like a ton of bricks? She was falling for him. Josie was sure he liked her. Was she right or was it his chivalrous care of her that she mistakenly took for attraction? One hour later she had one less question.

Jake suggested a walk to clear their heads. Shamus unhindered by a leash walked at his heels. He knew practically nothing about her. Had she left someone behind when she came here?

He asked her that very thing noting that he had caught her off guard. She looked at him knowing what he meant. "No," She replied. "There is no one waiting for my return." He hadn't thought so but anything was possible. He smiled at her. That made him even more pleased. "I took a couple of years off after my parents died." I didn't start college until I was well into my twenties. It took a long time to get my degree and by the time I hit thirty two which was only recently I stayed busy. Between work and school there was no time and to be honest not a lot of interest. I dated here and there but never anyone I clicked with. There were very few second dates."

He knew that one too well. He and Holly had never really clicked. He was not sure why they had even been together. Unfortunately that fact took two years to surface. His thirtieth birthday gift to himself was to walk away for good. At thirty six he was okay with where his life had went. He had tried to re-enter the dating scene but the longer he stalled the less important it became. Until last week that is. Until the day Ally walked into his life. They stopped at a two track lined by tall pines on either side. Jake took three bottles of water out of his knapsack. He handed one to her and before opening his own he uncapped the third and let it stream out for Shamus to lap up. She respected him for the way he put his needs before his own. It spoke volumes to his character.

Jake took her hand in his as they reached the clearing and took seats on a fallen tree. Ally held his eyes for several moments. What was he thinking? What was it behind those blue eyes that held her there? He bent and kissed her slowly and as she responded to him he kissed her more hungrily. She did not back away when he pulled her closer continuing his passionate taking of her lips, her tongue merged with his.

When he lifted his head she was breathless. His heart was racing like he had just ran a marathon. He had never felt that with anyone ever. It was a surge of electricity that he still could feel pulsing in his veins. Ally looked away. With her head lowered and her soft voice trembling she told him that if he did not stop she would find herself in love with him. Jake lifted her chin so she had to look into his eyes. "Too late for me," he said in a low husky tone. "I'm already in love with you." He kissed her again. Tenderly this time. "There is nothing I would not give and nothing I would not do for you."

They sat for a long time quietly each to their own thoughts. What would this mean in the bigger scheme of things? They had no idea what they were truly dealing with. Jake's company could be hurt in all of this. Ally could not let that happen. She was sure of only one thing. She had to find out who the other part of "they" was and what their role in Emma's life and death were. There was no way the two were not tethered. Jake glanced over at her. She was like himself lost in thought. Clara Finley was going to be trouble. He knew that without a doubt. Her vigilante tactics while paid in gossip and conjecture would still carry weight with a percentage of the townsfolk. He scoffed inwardly. Let her talk. She can't touch me. My reputation is solid. Ally was a whole separate issue. He told her as much. "She will keep this going as long as there is any hint of fuel. Mitchell, while being a stand-up guy, did you no favors by defending you." Ally agreed. There was raw contempt in that woman's expression as she had left. "So now what?" Jake gave her a small kiss as he helped her up. "I have no clue yet...but I will."

When they returned Jake gave Shamus fresh water and filled his food bowl. He grabbed a flavored dog biscuit and held it out to him.

He looked down at him. "Enjoy," he said as he leaned over to scratch his ears. Shamus had been with him since he was a pup. Now at six years old he could not imagine his life without him. "Would you feel safe here with him or would you rather go to the restaurant?" It was eleven thirty. He needed to meet Mike. When she didn't answer right away he wondered where her mind was. "I have to go." "I'm sorry. I know you do." As much as she wanted to see Josie Ally did not think she could take another scene of any kind and told him she would be fine with staying. "I won't be gone long," he assured. "No one will bother you here." He turned back as he got to the door. "There are a couple T Bones in the fridge. Why don't you make a side dish to go with them? I will grill them up when I get back. There is a rib eye in there also for him," looking over at the dog again. "He's earned it." She seems okay. It would do her good to busy herself in his absence and take her thoughts off of what was most likely eating at her. Her eyes found his. She knew he was trying to keep her occupied. She appreciated the effort. She said goodbye to him but he did not go just yet. He crossed the room and gave her a small kiss on the forehead. "Ally?" "Look at me." She raised her eyes to his. "I meant every word." She knew what he was saying. She nodded. "Me too."

Jake and Mike slipped in grateful that Joann was at work and they would not be interrupted. He acknowledged them and tried to sit up. "Hey," Mike said, "Don't do that on our account." Tim laid back on the pillow using the button to incline his position a little. His voice was low as he greeted them. He doesn't look so hot Jake thought. "We can do this another time," he told him. "Maybe you should rest." "NO!" His voice was vehement now. "You need to know Jake. There is evil in that house." He and Mike took a seat as Tim continued his tone more subdued. "I was on the last box furthest from the door when my attention was diverted by an icy cold blast of air. There should not have been one. It was eighty five degrees yesterday." He paused as a nurse came in to do a routine check of his vitals and give him his pain medicine. When she exited the room he began again. "I need to get this out before that little pill starts doing his magic."

"I went to go find the source and I was halfway across the attic when I heard it. A little girl's voice saying, "It is not nice. I will not do it." "It was immediately followed by a low wicked laugh of an old man." Jake and Mike both regarded him. They were thinking the same that Tim must have hit his head really hard when he landed. An old man? Jake took that in. Ally would have included that. When Tim realized he was being doubted he cast off the pain he was in and sat straight up looking directly at them his eyes alive with fear. "I was not hallucinating, I know doc said I have a concussion from hitting my head on the window sill but I heard it. I could smell his rancid breath Jake. As I was trying to make a run for it to get to you I was lifted off my feet sending me airborne with a force that was NOT from this world. When I landed beneath that window I felt my bone breaking and that is when I must have screamed." He motioned for Mike to hand him his water from the table. Jake couldn't wrap his head around it. Tim recognized it as skepticism. "I could smell him damn it!" Tim was not lying, he was not creating a new legend. As insane as it was Jake believed every word.

They left a few minutes later as he began to drift off under the dose he had been given. Mike broke the silence as they walked to the elevator telling him he was going to Hamilton's to get the new window. "I don't know Mike. Maybe you should give some more thought to this. I don't have any idea what is coming but I can guarantee you we haven't seen anything yet." He didn't know how he was so certain but he was. Mike gave him a sideways glance. "Tim will be okay soon but you my friend have your ass hanging out in the wind and I'm going to cover it." "Besides," he added with a trace of excitement in his voice, "This is the biggest thing that has happened here. I wouldn't miss one minute of it." Jake managed a small smile. He hoped Mike's excitement would not be replaced by terror in the days and weeks to come. What had they gotten themselves into? As he made the short drive back he contemplated on what he should tell her. He did not want to scare her any more than she was but he had no authority to keep any of the details from her. It was her home and she, alone, would have to decide what to do with the information he would give her.

Ally looked at the clock. Jake would be back soon. The seasoned steaks were on a platter to bring them to room temperature. She chose a potato from the pantry. After rinsing it she sliced it lengthwise, added salt and pepper and wrapped it in foil to cook along with the meat. She made a simple salad tossing it with an oil and vinegar dressing. There was nothing else to be done. She ventured out to the front porch and took a seat on one of the cushioned chairs to wait, Shamus at her side. When he pulled up he grabbed her bags out of the bed and called to the dog who ran to him wagging his tail. "Did you keep our girl safe," he asked. The dog barked once. "Of course you did."

As he lit the grill and took a chair beside it he called for Ally who was in the kitchen. She came out the slider and he asked her to sit with him. While dinner sizzled away he repeated everything Tim had said. He studied her. Her eyes widened. She had the same look as his friend. Palpable fear. Was that why Emma wanted help? Was this old man, whoever he was trying to harm her? Was she trying to escape some hold he had over her? "I honestly don't know," he said heavily. "Until the other night I did not believe in ghosts. Now I am...we are facing two of them." "I'm sorry. I can't put this on you. You didn't sign on for this." "Neither did you." "We talked about this Ally, I am not going anywhere." She smiled softly at him. He was too good to her. It was no wonder she loved him.

Jake held her as they lay on his bed trying to make some sort of plan of action. It wasn't going to be easy. They were not exactly dealing with the run of the mill problem. The easiest solution was for her to just leave the manor and its inhabitants behind but he knew she wouldn't even consider that. She had a deep need to discover what other secrets Emma and the house held. Especially, now, that the other entity had made himself known. He understood. He got it. Emma was, even though distant and adopted, her family and she would not walk away until this was over.

It was only seven but the last two days had taken their toll on her. She drifted off to sleep and Jake lie there his headache returning as he wondered what the hell he was doing. Yes he loved her as wild as that was and he believed her words earlier but as wonderful as that was love would not save them from spirits and ghosts. Around ten o'clock came the first in a series of nightmares. She began to toss fitfully moaning and then calling out to the little girl. "Emma come back!" "It's not safe!" "Ally?" Jake shook her. "Wake up." Shamus was at the bedside whimpering. "It's okay boy," he told him but the dog did not move. She screamed and opened her eyes. It was so real. She was shaking all over. Jake switched on the lamp. "Tell me." "I don't know," "She was in the woods walking towards the road in her nightgown. Maybe a dress considering the era." "She kept refusing telling me he was waiting for her." "I felt something behind me that I could not see. It reached for me and I screamed." "You sure did," he replied softly "but I am here, Ally, everything is fine." He gathered her into his arms. He felt her trembling still in the aftermath of the dream. "Trust in me Ally," he whispered as she moved closer to him. "I will get us through this." She was still in the cradle of his arms when they awoke just before dawn.

CHAPTER SEVEN

Looking For Answers

"Not today boy," he told Shamus. Today you stay here in the air," "We have business and I can't leave you in the truck that long." The dog padded back down the hallway and laid down. It was sweltering. He and All both wore shorts, light shirts and sneakers. There was no need to dress other than the most comfortable that they could. He explained as he held open her door that he was taking her to see Father James. He had not been to mass in ages but they were going to need more advice than any ordinary person could provide at this minute.

He led them into his study. Jake and his aunt had been members since he was a boy. He had not seen him in quite a while but it wasn't his place to ask and from what he had told him on the phone his confessions and attendance would not be addressed today. He sat there his fingers resting on his Bible as he listened, giving up silent prayers as he did so. When Jake finished he gave up a final request to his

Lord to give him strength and the ability to guide them on this road. He had seen many unusual things in his sixty five years and had heard many priests speak of this. Seminars had been held for situations as these but he never imagined he would wind up in the middle of one. When he finally spoke he recited "God be with us." Jake and Ally both made the sign of the cross with him, their faces solemn. "I have heard the talk over the years about Morley Manor but the only actual evidence of anything was the death of the child."

"I, too, Ally looked up it up a long time back when I first came here back in the early seventies. My parishioners were looking to me to put the story to rest. Every now and again someone would talk of seeing lights when there should have been none. Seeing apparitions in the attic window...so I did some checking but found nothing except for her tragic end." "I tried speaking to Sebastian but he was not acceptable to bringing up the past. He flat out told me to go away and not return." "I didn't take offense. How could I? He started out a young life with many responsibilities, too much for a man his age to handle and suffered enough for a lifetime already. I had no right to pursue him and I stopped." "I did learn, however from some of the old timers that

Emma Morley was actually the daughter of Evelyn Morley. She was over a decade his senior when they married. She only lived a short time after their wedding." Ally nodded telling him she knew that she had died during childbirth. "Anyway, I told them that it was just the imaginations of the fickle mind and nothing to worry on so hard. Before yesterday and Tim's accident which we now know was an experience from another realm most of them accepted my findings."

He sighed. He advised them that their first order would be going through old deeds at the county hall of record to learn who had owned the house before Sebastian. That, in itself may shed some light. The internet was a precious tool and would also be a good source to try digging up any facts about the previous owner. It would be limited, of course, unless it had been of significant news or value. Records only went back so far even there.

"Do you think the manor is possessed," Ally asked him. "I'm not sure. I would need more to go on than what we currently have. This may require an exorcism if so but that is a delicate thing and a request that does not come without strict guidelines or permission from someone higher up than myself." "This could be a simple haunting but unfortunately what you have told me does not support that." Jake and Ally shook his hand as he walked them out. They arranged another date after they had gained what they could in Rock Port and would see him then. They stopped in to see Josie and have lunch. A few of the people gave her looks but she ignored them. Her backbone would have to be stronger than to crumple at glares. He gave his aunt a small hug. He had missed her these past few days. She looked worried. She took off her apron and called to Midge in the back and told her she had the floor for a while and then joined them. "It's okay," Ally assured her. "It will work out." She was making promises she couldn't keep but it was worth it to see the small relief in Josie's eyes. She started to ask about Tim but Jake gave a barely perceptible shake of his head. Not here. Not now.

They made general conversation while they ate. A salad for her and a patty melt for him. He gave Josie a knowing look. "How about you closing up early on Saturday. We would like you and Mitchell to have dinner at my place." "Mike Moore," he said a little louder to catch the attention of those he knew were listening, "will be joining us." To hell with them. If they needed something to talk about he had just given it to them. Josie accepted. We? She regarded the two of them and after a moment a big smile came across her face. They were together. Jake knew what she was thinking. He gave her a wink and nodded. She was elated. Despite her current troubles and despite Jake's usual pattern of avoiding women they had found themselves in love. It did not matter to her that it wasn't possible. It did not matter that it was too soon. The heart wants what it wants she told herself. As they got up to go Josie gave Alley a big squeeze. "I am delighted," she told her in a hushed whisper, "Jake will be good for you and you for him." Had he told his aunt? He must have. She gave the woman a smile. "Thank you Josie, we will see you at six then?" "With bells on," was her reply.

On Saturday by six thirty the five of them were enjoying drinks on the back deck. It was a nice evening with cooler temperatures and they were taking full advantage of it. Mike manned the grill on which he put a load of brats and burgers on. Josie brought her famous potato salad, Mitchell a case of beer which they had on ice in the cooler. Jake moved his chair closer to Ally taking her hand and kissing it. He wanted his friends to know that they were a couple but without having to make any sort of announcement. His point was well taken. Mike smiled, Mitchell laughed. Jake Madden bitten by the elusive love bug. He never thought he would see the day. Go figure. He liked the duo alignment, however. He like Ally a lot and he had known Jake forever. It was a good alliance. They both were heading into the unknown and it was good they had each other to count on.

As they ate he went over their conversation with Father James. Mike whistled softly. Mitchell and Josie listened intently without interruption. When he finished he addressed Mike. "If you have any second thoughts, get out now," he told him. Mike shrugged. "I have more time than brains," he replied. He was not going to leave Jake hanging. Had Tim been able he would be on his side as well. That brought a round of laughter, real unforced glee that they had not felt in days. Jake outlined their plan as Ally and Josie cleared away dinner, Shamus waiting patiently for his treats which he knew were coming. Ally filled his bowl and added two burgers to it to which the dog gave her a sloppy lick wagging his tail.

He and Ally would go Monday to Rock Port to search the records. Mike, if he was still certain would finish the bathroom but at first sign of anything unusual he was to get out. No questions asked. He also said he had been able to hire on two guys from the next town. Mike asked who and was relieved to hear he knew of them. They were solid and he could count on them. "Put the other two on stripping the wall paper in the sitting room." "And Mike," he added in a no nonsense tone, "No one and I mean no one is to go up those stairs for any reason whatsoever." Mike was only too happy to oblige. "What about me," Mitchell asked, "is there something I should do?" Jake gave a deep sigh before answering. "If there is more coming our way it is going to get ugly around here. Better order more windows." He looked back to see if they had been overheard but Ally was still busy. He did not want her to know and doubted he would ever tell her. The people here were a good bunch.

He knew most of them since childhood but there were those, like Clara Finley and her crowd that could make life impossible if they saw the chance.

CHAPTER EIGHT

George Henry

"Good morning beautiful," Jake said as she and Shamus came down the hall. She was wearing a thin night shirt with a pair of shorts. Her long hair for once was loose and messy from sleep. He thought it was an amazing look on her. He had stayed up most of Saturday night after their guests left about midnight thinking about her. He had not made any references to her going to sleep in the spare room, the ever vigilant Shamus at her side. He would have preferred her to be in his bed but they were not to that stage and he would respect any boundaries spoken or unspoken that she put up. Sunday they took another long walk and spent the day quiet for the most part. They did not talk of Monday or what they may learn. They did not speak of spirits or evil or anything that had happened thus far. They instead, took that time to relax and have some sense of normality while it was still available to them.

Ally smiled at him. "Good morning to you as well." "Breakfast?" "I don't think I can eat," she replied "nerves I guess." He came to her then. "Ally, it is going to be alright. No matter what happens or what we find today we are in this together." She knew he was right. They could not change whatever may or may not be waiting for them to uncover but they would have each other to lessen the blow.

Shamus, again stayed behind. Ally dressed in white shorts and a blue top and him in black jeans and short sleeved button down headed off for Rock Port. His hand covered hers as he drove. He stole a glance at her. Her hair was still down. He liked that. The sun coming through the windshield was highlighting the auburn tints in it. She looked radiant. He only wished that radiance had reached her eyes. They were deep brown today, lost in thought. Uncertainty behind them. He wanted to take that from her and replace it with happiness but for the time being he had no control over anything nor the power to instill that in her.

This was tedious. Ally opened another large book. The net was of no use to them. It would be a long morning of going through each of the records from the late eighteen hundreds. They were not even sure of the years they needed to concentrate on. Jake decided they should go in logical formation. If Sebastian had bought the property sometime close to his eighteen birthday that would have been in nineteen twenty seven or eight he estimated. "Only look for entries before then and work backwards. We don't know how many had lived on the grounds so it will be a process of elimination." "Every entry we find will have to be researched until we come up with a viable candidate." Ally scrunched her nose up at him. He gave her a smile. "Back at it," he directed as he, himself, took a book off of the stack.

An hour and a half later Ally called his name. "Jake, I think I found it." "George Henry." "How can you be sure," he asked peering over her shoulder. "We have not even looked at anyone yet." The date and name were barely legible. The ink had begun to fade. George Henry – April Twentieth, Eighteen Hundred and Ninety Four. Jake rubbed his jaw, he needed a shave. How could she be so certain? Any number of people may have settled there after the civil war. Seeing his name in the ledger did not mean he was the culprit. He, too, may have had follies of his own that he had not bargained on when he paid a whopping two hundred dollars for the property. "It's him Jake. George Henry." "Ally?" "I got sick to my stomach when I looked at it. It's him."

They then looked up the man himself. That required going through public birth and death notices. He may not have even been from this area. Finally, the internet. They grabbed a fast lunch at the drive through of a fast food chain and went to the county library. George Henry - Born January Sixth, Eighteen Hundred Sixty Four in Suffolk County Virginia. A Civil War baby. Died November Fifth Nineteen?...wait the same year Sebastian took it over? He sold the property and in a few months' time expired? Of what? Natural causes? A bit more digging into what little there was in the archives produced the rest of the puzzle.

He commissioned the manor in fall of 1894 and resided there until his death from a house fire in twenty seven. The property passed to his deceased business partner's son...Sebastian Morley. There was the connection. Jake and Ally mulled this over. They went to the desk and asked the librarian if she knew of anyone who may still be around from those days that they could speak with. After a bit of checking she gave them the name of Silas Unger. He was in the nursing home just outside of Rock Port. She told them he was in his early nineties but he may be able to recall enough to help them. "Well. Do you want to see him," Jake asked already knowing her answer.

They stopped at the nurse's station and explained the reason for their visit and asked if Silas were up to seeing them. The older of them laughed. "He would be tickled pink. He doesn't get much company." When Ally asked if he was still of sound mind she rolled her eyes and laughed again. "That old coot can remember everything. He may be well on his way to being a century old but it has not dampened his love for women or gossip." She led them down to the community room and pointed him out. "Dinner is at five. Until then he is all yours."

Silas Unger. His hair long gone, his skin speckled with age spots motioned them over with a bony finger when he heard his name. What were these two wanting from him? No matter, he thought, any company is better than none at all. The days were dull and mundane even for him. He welcomed them in a shaky but polite voice. Jake introduced them and asked if they could sit with him. "No need to ask," Silas told them, "you got any chewing gum?" Ally fished in her purse. She handed him an unopened pack she had purchased at Mitchells last week. He shoved it into the pocket of his pants. "I will save this for later," he whispered. "If they knew then I'd have to be sharing it all." They both smiled at the old man. He had spunk that was for sure.

"George Henry," he began after a moment. "Now that is a name I haven't heard in years. Many years. He died in that house you know?" "I still recall the way it was," he began as his mind drifted back to a different time. Jake squeezed Ally's hand. Answers. That's what they had been hoping to find and here it was in the elderly gentleman. "He was a mean man you know? Always muttering, always yelling at us kids to get off of his property. We used to fish down to the creek which really was a small river." Jake did know, about the creek anyhow. How many times had he, Tim and Mike traversed the woods instead of taking the tracks to the trestle? How many times had they walked the tracks themselves? Or drink beers down there out of the watchful sight of parents? He was sure the teens of this generation still used it as a hangout.

Silas went on as the two of them listened closely not wanting to miss one iota of whatever he would tell them. "Anyhow, we did as he said but we always went back. He didn't catch us every time." The old man snickered, "We got by him lots." Jake and Alley laughed in spite of themselves. Silas sure was a character. "I was young. Eight, ten, no more than though. House caught a fire one night. Only hurt the big room but he got that smoke in his body and he was done for." Jake started a question but Silas was not finished. "I heard my momma and grandma talking. You know how it is with kids. We like to know everything about everything. Specially' back in those days. Very different time. Any news was big news." Ally thought he had said that last part wistfully. How many changes had he seen in his lifetime? "My grandma said the fire was confusing the volunteer fire department which is all we had. Something to do with the creosote built up in the chimney. They first ruled it as a chimney fire and he got all the smoke that backed up onto the downstairs. House was solid you know? Only thing burned which was that closest to the hearth which caught the drapes n all. He was old. Bad lungs they said."

Jake and Ally both were puzzled. How is that confusing? "Done heard her say a few months later that Doyle down to the mill said he heard there was no creosote up the chimney and doubted there was much more than in the cleanout." They were getting it now. He also told bragged that he had it on good word that the flue had been shut." Silas sniffed. "Nothing ever came of it. It was different then." "What was news one day was a rumor the next and it all went away." Murder?

Sebastian's father? Impossible he was gone. "His business partner," Ally asked when he finished speaking, did you know him and his family?" "No." "I lived more over to here. I took long walks. Mighty long walks to see my pals." Jake smiled. The old man was cool. A small Ding. Ding. Ding came over the loudspeaker. Dinner. Five o' clock. On their way out Jake was stopped by a middle aged nurse. "Aren't you Josie's boy?" He corrected her, "My aunt." "I thought so, my cousin goes to her church." Jake smiled politely. "Can you do me a favor?" He took out his wallet and handed her a twenty dollar bill. "Can you see to it that Silas is kept in gum? She returned the smile. "He likes Beechnut best."

There was much to talk about. They had hit the jackpot. Why then were they not saying anything? Why did she have that look on her face? She should have been thrilled but as he saw the proof in her eyes he knew she was far from. The drive back was quiet. Too quiet. What was she thinking? He did not try to get her to talk about it. She would tell him when she was ready and he would wait until she was. It had been one long day after another mentally lately. She had a right to be in her head. Shamus walked, dinner or the leftovers rather all cleared away Jake sat down next to her on the sofa

"Tell me." "Can ghosts," there was not even an inkling of a question that they were real in her mind now..."Can they remember? Do they really haunt to seek revenge or it is they just are still here?" He kissed her lightly, put his arm around her and pulled her to him. "Ally, last week if you would have asked me this I would have thought you were out of it." She nodded resting against him with her eyes closed. Another headache. "Now?" "What am I supposed to tell you? Why don't you just ask me if you can smell them? If they can injure you...because I do not sanely have those answers either." He had not wanted to sound that harsh but these were not typical conversation and there was no delicacy in this. "I know." "What is it that you know Ally?" "That I should not even have to be asking anything. That there should be no Emma. No George Henry and no problem."

Shamus was whimpering, pawing at him. Ally! His feet barely touched the stairs. He turned the hall light on. She was moaning. He watched her. She began to cry and then to thrash about screaming. "NO!" "YOU LEAVE HER BE GEORGE HENRY!" "NO NO!" Jake had her in his arms within seconds cradling her, quietly arousing her. It was no easy task but scaring her more by yelling or shaking her was not going to help. "Shh... Ally," he soothed. "We're here." Her trusty new best friend at her side. She stopped crying. She opened her eyes. "Oh Jake," "I'm sorry. I was ..." "I know." "Emma." She was calling to her for help again. This time she was being shadowed by George Henry. Ally could see him. Could hear him. Could smell him.

"He is hideous Jake. If you took all of the hatred in the world and put it in that face it still wouldn't come close to a description. It was beyond imagination. Beyond explanation." Ally was terrified. It clung to her. He had seen her afraid before but this was not that. Pure terror in her eyes, in the way her body trembled and hands shook. "He was shadowing us. I would not let Emma leave. Jake it was putrid. His breath." She gagged. He thought of Tim. "I could smell him damn it..." "I was challenging him. That is when he showed himself. She shuddered again. "Why were you screaming NO, NO?" "Did he take her?" She gulped and shuddered again. Jake held her tightly. "No." A barely heard, "Emma said...I am next." "George Henry needs new friends." He slid in bed beside her. Shamus between them and the hall. "I'm sorry Ally." She was sheet white. "Don't be afraid. I got you." Did he? All he could do was pray that he did. "He is coming for me Jake."

The longest night so far. Ally had a breakdown. It was almost six in the morning. She still was in fetal position in his arms when he opened his eyes. He pulled the sheets up over her grateful sleep had found her. That nightmare scared the hell out of her! Out of him! How was he coming? A haunting? An accident? Ally opened her eyes. "No," she whispered, "He wants...me." What the hell? He thought she was sleeping. How did she know? He had not said that out loud.

She was silent. She was withdrawn and she was inconsolable.

CHAPTER NINE

Mental Health Week

It was Wednesday. He had not spoken to Mike which meant no news was great news. He had hardly spoken to Ally. She was still shut down. They went through the motions but the charade of the last day and a half was wearing on him. Another nightmare but no recall. Where would this end? Shamus was her second skin. The dog knew. He could barely get her to eat. Hell he barely got himself to eat. This was insane. Out of the box. Out of this world. Out of your mind insane. He put in another call to Father James. After hearing of the latest developments he gave the sign of the cross. "I want to take her in but I am worried that they will think she has lost her mind and admit her. She hasn't. She is just in a really bad place right now." After a moment's thought he told him to just keep her close and watch her. "A doctor, at this point, Jake won't do Ally much good." A possession? He

would have to ask about it being sanctioned.
If they would sanction one. "I will speak to my
superiors." "It will take a bit of time."
"Until then God be with you."

Thursday night she seemed better. They
ordered in a pizza from a local proprietor new
to the area. As they ate Ally apologized for
being such a lump the past few days but
admitted she was scared. She did not know what
George Henry wanted but that he was coming for
her. Jake regarded her silently. He was
thinking about his talk with Father James. Was
Ally really in the beginning stages of
possession? Was it the house itself? He did
not know anything except that she was going to
go nowhere near the manor until he did.
"Jake?" "I wouldn't blame you if you changed
your mind." "About?" Ally looked at him.
"This, you, me...all of it." She, like he had
Mike, was trying to let him off the hook. He
did not even consider taking her up on it
rather he was angry for it even being a
question. He was angry for all of the things
he had no idea of how to fix. Could it be
fixed? "I'm staying," he said in a tone that
told her not to offer again.

Friday and Saturday went just as badly as they
had earlier in the week. More nightmares. No
recall...just terror. Sunday morning she

greeted Jake quietly. He blanched. It was not her voice. It was sing song. Child-like. He sat there unmoving. "Emma?" She turned to him and smiled. It was not Ally's smile. It was immature, silly and gone just as quickly as it came. As was Emma. "Jake?" He looked strange. He jumped up and went to her. "Ally?" Was it her? Damn it what was going on? "Jake, what is the matter with you. I'm the one seeing ghosts and yet you look like you have too." No way was he telling her one bit of it. "Oh. I'm sorry. I was just in my head I guess."

He watched her like a clock. He wished Shamus had not been outside. He would have known she was coming. It was her. He didn't have to see her as Ally did. He had no doubt. Mike called breaking into his thoughts. The floors were cured, the tiles removed and the wall paper stripped. What now? "I will be there in the morning," he told Mike. "We can decide then." Before he hung up he asked Mike to remind Tim to get the comp papers turned in and to not worry about wages lost. He would pay him in full up front while he waited out the standard ten days. It was the very least he could do. He felt the weight of the world was on him at this second. He had no idea of what now. Ally, Tim, Mike and now...Emma.

They walked Shamus back to the same two track. They sat on the same fallen log. Jake took her hand in his. "It's been one long week," he said quietly. "How are you holding up?" Ally looked his way. "I'm fine now," she lied. He looked awful. She had put him through the wringer. His eyes told that he had not slept well lately. His brows were constantly furrowed in deep thought or worry. Jake groaned. "Ally, you don't have to pretend." "I'm not. I am fine now." "You are going to the manor tomorrow?" "If so, I think I can go with you." So that was it. She was lying to try to be able to discover more. "I can't let that happen." Was he worried she may be hurt like Tim? "I don't know Ally," he replied. His favorite line. I don't know. "If it means that much to you then I will stay but...If nothing happens over the next couple days I want to be there." It was the best compromise he was going to get and he knew it. He nodded in agreement wondering how he would put her off next.

Later as she showered he called Josie. Could she get Midge and her husband Big Al to cover the day shift until further notice? When his aunt asked why he had no option but to say, "She has been acting strangely. She is not herself. Literally." Josie replaced the receiver and she, too, made the sign of the cross. The outcome was that she would keep her busy, take her out and take her anywhere but to town. Ally was none the wiser when Jake said she would be there to hang out with her and to get to know her nephew's girlfriend better. She actually smiled. A tiny fib to see that smile was worth it. He could not tell her the truth. He would not tell her that it was for her own safety or that he could not risk leaving her alone. If he had he said all that then he would have to open the other door and he was not about to. Not right now.

When she was ready to turn in Jake anticipated his next move. He would sleep on the couch. He would be closer if he needed to get to her fast. What if she...no, she would not become Emma as she slept. He prayed on that. He closed his eyes wondering if tonight would be the one where he got some sleep of his own. He could have easily just said yes that he changed his mind. She wouldn't even have held it against him. He could have taken the coward's way out and told her that it was just too much and that it was better to do it now then later. Jake Madden, however, was no coward and he had promised that he would stick by her. Loving her made it all the more difficult. He had to think about every move now to ensure her safety. He could not have her babysat forever. He knew her. She would force him to make good on his compromise of going to the manor. In reality, as if reality existed lately, he could not stop her if she went against his wishes. He could not do one damn thing about it.

CHAPTER TEN

The Journal

He said goodbye to Ally and Josie and called for Shamus. He wanted him with him on this day. His aunt after breakfast would be taking her to the open air flea market they held in Rock Port that started the first Monday in August. Good grief, it was August already. The dog leapt up into the passenger seat of the cab and they were off. "It looks great Mike," he said. It really did. Mike had outdone himself. He shook hands with the two others Curtis and Rod and thanked them for helping out. Mike told him they were thinking that maybe they could start re mortaring the fireplace stones but Jake wanted him to install the floodlights and have them work on the paper Ally had picked out for the sitting room. It was a deep moss but with slight sheen that would grace the large room well. The three side by side windows would keep it bright enough to offset its deepness. When that was finished then he wanted to get some lunch for all their work. While they were doing that he was going to give the attic a good combing. He could not put it off any longer. Mike asked if he should go as well but Jake patted the Rottweiler and said half joking, "I think I have all I need." He gave Mike a look and reminded him to heed the instructions he had been given a week ago. He understood.

Jake unlatched the hook listening, watching Shamus but the dog remained in place silent. He cautiously opened the door and went in. It was the same as he remembered it except that the pool of blood was now just a dried stain beneath the window. He would come up after with disinfectant and a scrub brush. If she were to come back that is not what he wanted her to see. He went through the two trunks. Nothing. A dusty old doll and some old wooden hangers in one and the other books. He took one out and wiped it to see its title. School books. Emma Morley. Multiplication tables. He thumbed through it but there were no hidden secrets just pages of scribbled math problems consistent with a child her age. The rest of them were much the same. English. Handwriting. He replaced them and closed the lids. That was a letdown. He had hoped to find something amongst the cobwebs. He would get rid of those too.

He left the door open. No sense in trying to get the hook off with a bucket and brush in his hands. When he returned fifteen minutes later Shamus alerted to the floor. There sat the doll. How in blazes? He had not even taken it out. Had he? No he knew he didn't. He hadn't even given it more than a quick look. He was perplexed but not worried. The dog sat patiently at his heels waiting on him. No sign of impending danger. Jake made fast work of the stain and then went back down but not before putting the doll back in its trunk and securing the door. He would not say anything to Mike but when they were done today, all work was going to stop. For how long he couldn't say. What reason would he give Ally? He still had a few hours to come up with one. Over lunch of chili dogs and fries which the four of them scarfed like mad he told Mike of his decision. He told the three of them they would be getting paid at the end of the day and if they wanted to resume work when it was time they were more than welcome. It was agreeable to all three but Mike wondered what had happened that Jake was not saying.

Ally, meanwhile was elbow deep in sweet corn. Jake would surely love to have it with dinner. It was shaping up to be a good day. This is what I needed she told herself. Fresh air and to be surrounded by a lot of people. It felt...normal. How long had it been since that had happened? Josie was great company. She introduced her here and there to a few people she knew. They seemed nice enough but they were not from Edgerton. Had they been she was positive they would not have been so friendly towards her. Josie asked her if she had ever canned or put up vegetables. She relayed that her grandmother had but she never found the time to try it out. "I will teach, you will learn." Ally laughed. It felt so good to laugh. Their next stop was the strawberry farm. Ally had never been to one. "OHH," Josie said excitedly, "It is a real treat. You get to pick your own or buy them by the quarts pre-packaged." "Out there," she told her pointing at the rows of low plants bursting with red berries, "are the best ones." So be it then. They would pick strawberries. She wondered if Josie had a recipe for good jam. She laughed. "What do you think you get on your toast when you come to breakfast."

Back to work. He may as well help with the final two walls. Mike asked about the masonry again. Jake deliberated and said they should clean the interior first. That would be a job in itself. "Have you ever seen a fireplace with that depth and width?" Mike said he had not.

After a minute more he decided it and the stones could wait until the chimney had been done. There had been a fire here and who knows how many fires had been lit since with no special logs to burn the creosote. Mike smiled at him. "Did it Tuesday. Took the brush down it, swept the clean out after what fell." Jake was about to hand him his hide for not only going up the ladder but climbing onto the unstable roof. Mike read it and countered, "Hey I was bored. Sue me." Jake gave in. "If you get the interior spic and span with no soot at all we will talk about the stones. Yes, he was going to be able to put his skill to use. He loved working with stone and these ones were mixed sizes and variation. He couldn't wait. There were about a dozen that needed to be re-set. "And Mike," he added, "be careful will you?" He flung him a look of who me? Jake smiled. "Yes, You!" He looked over at Shamus who was sleeping on the floor. He was jealous that he was not doing that exact thing.

It was getting late but since Mike had made good on the interior he was going to wait it out with him and let him take the two hours or so to complete it. That way at least the fireplace as a whole was done and so were they. At least for now. At six he let Curtis and Rod go cash in hand and told him they would talk soon. They waved and were out the door leaving just him and Mike. He told him about the doll. "It did not pan out to anything but of course you would have known that by now." Mike nodded. He trusted Jake. He would not put him deliberately in harm's way. "Wish I knew what to say," Mike told him as he set one of the upper stones in place. Jake wished he did too. "Mike, how in the hell is this even happening? We grew up laughing at this and now, look at us. Trying to decipher what a ghost's next move will be." Mike did not know any more than he did.

Jake called Ally. Josie answered and said they had a terrific day and that she was fine. "Where is she Josie, I want to talk to her." Josie calmed him. She was right there. "Ally?" He let out his breath. "Hi Jake." She told him of where they had been and did he like corn on the cob? He said yes that he did and tomorrow would be better for it. He was going to be a while still. She was fine with that. He silently thanked his aunt. She had done wonders with her. She sounded like herself again. "Do you want me to pick something up?" "I can still get a take out." She told him three Club Sandwiches on Rye would do the trick. He said he would call it in when they were almost done. "I love you Ally," he told her quietly as they were hanging up. "I know Jake. Thankyou."

Two stones to go. He called the restaurant and placed his order. Mike was going to Tim's and wanted nothing. He had an envelope of cash for himself and one that was for his brother and he would see he got it tonight. Shamus looked positively happy lying there blissfully snoring away. He couldn't wait until bedtime. If he was not awaken by Ally...or Emma again. The last stone. Mike wiggled it and as it gave way from the last vestiges that held it he pulled it out slowly. It was on the third to last sequence and he was down on his knees peering into the opening as he took it out. "What is that?" "What is what?" "Hang on," he told him and reached inside. There in the very back of the opening was a medium sized leather book. Mike pulled it out gingerly. It looked old. He handed it wordlessly to Jake who opened the cover. "Finish that one or leave it, I really don't care right now." Mike applied the mortar to it and slid it into place sealing it with more. Jake was holding open the page for him to see. My Findings – Sebastian Morley. 1929.

Neither spoke until they and Shamus were at the drive. "What are you going to do with it?" He believed he already knew. "I have to give it to her.   I just don't want to do it tonight."   Mike looked at his friend.   That dude needed some rest, badly.   He would not tell a soul, not even Tim.   This was Jake's call.   Jake extended his hand "Thanks Mike. For everything."   Mike shook it and told him to watch his ass.   No problem there he thought. Just another to add to the list.

He fed Shamus and then set out the Styrofoam containers.   Ally grabbed some napkins and Josie brought out a pitcher of water and ice. He half listened as Josie told him how Ally had never been to the fields before. "She is a real pro.   We got the biggest sweetest berries." Jake had his mind elsewhere.   In the cab of his truck lay Sebastian's Journal and he was keeping it from her.   How was that going to play out?   He had no right.   It was her property.   He said goodnight to his aunt and thanked her for being there. "We managed to finish so I'm going to be around the next few days.   I have to check on another site but that can wait."   Josie hugged Ally and gave Shamus a rub.   He was sitting at Ally's feet and had been since they arrived.

Jake was out the second he knew Ally was sleeping soundly.   Shamus would let him know. It was about four am when he was awakened. What was that noise?   Where was Shamus? Why didn't he bark? He rubbed his eyes and walked towards it. It was coming from outside. The door was slightly ajar. He opened it a bit more and reached out the screen for the porchlight as he came out. What the hell? Shamus waiting outside the truck and Ally with the interior light on was reading the journal. Jake crossed over to them. She was not even startled. She knew he would be coming. She left the door open so he wouldn't wake and took Shamus with her so he wouldn't alert. "You should have told me Jake," she said in a small voice. He was speechless. There was no possible way she knew it was there. None at all! He took the book from her and led her back into the house. As he sat her down on the sofa he asked her how she knew. "I do not know but...I did."

This was the second time she had knowledge of things she should not have. She had read his mind that night. There was no other explanation and in light of all this would that even surprise him? Would anything? He was on a limb here. "Did ...Did Emma tell you?" Ally replied after a moment that she did not think so. "I don't remember dreaming tonight. I was asleep and then I was going out with Shamus." He put his head in his hands and prayed. "How much did you read?" "How far did you get?" "Only the first three pages. His thoughts of his wife Evelyn." Jake took her hand. This was way past anything he had answers for. She should not have been out there. She should not have known but she was and she did. "Please let it wait until tomorrow," he asked her quietly. "Ally," "I'm worried about you." She nodded and went back into her room. Jake was right behind them. "If you sleep here. I sleep here. My bed or yours?"

"You choose but you are not leaving my sight."

CHAPTER ELEVEN

Words from The Past

She was next to him when he woke up. His arms still holding her to make sure. He watched her as she slept. At least she was peaceful. He was thankful for that and decided he was going to stay right there in bed most of the day as soon as he let Shamus out. He was mentally tore up. How had she known? He couldn't get it off of his mind. The dog followed him outside after getting food and water. Jake watched him as he ran around the yard. He had been her partner in crime last night. He wanted to be mad but he couldn't. Technically he had been keeping guard. When they came in he tossed him a biscuit and the two of them went back to Ally's room where she still lie sleeping. He crawled in beside her and closed his eyes.

Later that afternoon curled up on the sofa, Jake next to her with Shamus at her feet Ally opened the journal. She skipped over the pages she had already gone over. On the fourth page dated July 20, 1929 Sebastian wrote of Emma and every entry thereafter.

I think my child, Evelyn's child is showing signs of the affliction that held her mother. She no longer goes out to play. She should be out in the sun riding her beloved sorrel Mist. She seems to prefer to be inside most day and that is troubling.

August 4, 1929 –

Mrs. Frank our dedicated housekeeper and cook has come to me with disturbing news. Emma no longer wishes to go out at all and has been found in the attic playing with a doll that I do not know where it hails from. I would not worry but for her tea set lies unused. She has no desire for her once love of dress up. I have taken account of this and shall watch her. I am so young. I have no notion of what to do with her.

August 15, 1929 –

Perhaps I am looking for trouble where none lies. It has rained all week and the child has gone back to her normal habits and seems quite content.

Jake looked at over at Ally. She was certain there would be something here but would not miss one paragraph. One entry. Had it been him he may have just given most of a quick glance to get to the ending but in view of all that was going on she was probably taking the right approach. It was important to understand what Sebastian was worried over and what Emma would do in or out of context next.

August 22, 1929 –

School will be in session soon. We have taken Emma to town to buy her the best I can afford in shoes and clothing. She is beautiful just as my darling Evelyn. She looks so much like her I can hardly bear it.

August 30, 1929 –

The child has not been herself these past days. She is no longer happy but moody and morose. What had brought this change in her? She no longer sings and jumps her hoop. She no longer smiles. I am coming to accept that my first thoughts were correct. Has Evelyn's sickness come to prey on the child?

Ally stopped then. "Jake, he thinks Emma is mentally ill. That is what Evelyn's affliction was." He nodded. That was the only possible meaning. "I think George Henry is near." "He is causing the change in her."

September 2, 1929

Mrs. Frank has exposed that she had not been able to locate Emma at noon meal. She found her in the attic again with that same doll. When she was called upon the child did not answer. I cannot have her rude or disobedient. I must speak with her. She must stop this nonsense. It has carried on too long. She still is quiet, given to fits of crying. A doctor may be needed in the next days.

September 10, 1929 -

My sweet Emma has told me she has a new friend but that I cannot see or hear him. When I ask her what is the name of her new and imaginary friend she will only say she cannot tell me. That it is a secret. I suppose it is not so out of form. She is secluded here beyond school. She has no children to gather with. Perhaps it is I who is going daft in thinking the worst.

September 12, 1929 -

Mrs. Frank tells me she thinks it is not good for Emma to be in the attic all day when she is not at her studies. It burdens her that she will only talk to her new friend. She says it is not right and that she must find another way to occupy her time. She has caught her in deep conversation with him. What should I do? Should

I take her under my wing and find an interest we could share

together? If only my work were not so pressing.

   September 15, 1929 –

The household was awakened by Emma. Mrs. Frank aroused me to say that when she checked on her the child was not in her bed but found her in the attic again in the dark talking to whoever she had dreamed up. I have spoken with her and made it clear that there would be no more late night visits to that room. When I pleaded to know why she was in there she would only say he was waiting for her. I am in distress. This cannot continue. Mrs. Frank is right. This is not healthy.

Ally closed the book. "I do not feel well." Jake suggested dinner may settle her stomach but Ally shook her head. "No, I couldn't eat." She stood and made her way down the hall. "I need to lie down." Jake was immediately concerned. She was perfectly fine an hour ago. He followed them and questioned her further. "Maybe the flu has caught me," she said in a tired voice. He doubted that but anything was possible. She was asleep within minutes. He turned on a lamp just before dark. How long had he been sitting there? He went to see if she was awake and found that she was still out. He called to Shamus and gave him his dinner and then took him out the back leaving the slider open so he could hear if she stirred.

Ten o' clock. She had been dead to the world for hours. Maybe she really was coming down with something. He showered, shaved and put on a pair of shorts before looking in on her again. No change. Shamus looked up at him as if to say he would be on watch. That dog, he thought, is more human than most people he knew. He turned out the lamp and laid down. The journal still on the table untouched since she had left it there. As much as he wanted to go through it he would not. He would wait for her.

He awoke to Shamus growling. He was not in the house. Jake ran to the open door. It had been raining. She was soaking wet. The Rottweiler had her by the sleeve and was pulling her back. What on earth? Jake ran to her. "Stand down!" The dog let her go but put himself in front of her now and began to growl again baring his teeth at some unseen adversary just up beyond the patch of trees. Jake reached her just as she passed out. He had her in his arms and yelled at Shamus to stop. "Stand down," he repeated. The dog did not obey for a moment and then after a third time he growled once more and was silent. He was at his master's side as he carried her into the house and laid her on the sofa.

"Ally," Jake prodded harshly. "Wake up!" She moaned and opened her eyes disoriented, tried to stand and then began to throw up. He ran to get towels and a glass of water. What was she doing out there? What was his dog going nuts over? Shamus had seen or felt something. He threw a wet towel onto the wood floor and then scooped her up and carried her in to the bathroom where he held her head a s she began to get sick again. When the nausea passed he handed her a cool washcloth and told her to put it on her forehead and to not move. He went into her room and got out a set of pajamas and returned. He stripped her of the wet clothing turning the shower on and coaxing her into it. He got in with her heedless to having shorts on. Heedless to her nakedness. He used the spray nozzle to rinse her off and then washed her hair.

What had just happened? He turned off the shower and grabbed the robe on the hook. It was too big for her but he paid that no mind. She was crying now. Sobbing. "Ally, please don't cry. It's okay." Was it? Was anything? He wrapped her in the robe and guided her to her room setting her on the edge of the bed and told her to stay there and he would be right back. He whistled for Shamus and took the dog outside after turning on the floodlight. He went towards the spot Shamus had alerted on but found nothing. Silence. No sound. No one there. The dog was not in error. Whatever was there although gone he had seen as an enemy or intruder. He was sure of that. He locked the door behind him and went back to Ally who was exactly as he had left her. She was no longer crying but she looked as if the tears would start again any second. She had no recollection of being out in the rain. She had not one idea of why she would have been. "What is happening to me Jake," she asked in a tiny voice. The dreaded phrase..."I don't know."

Long after she was settled and sleeping again he cleaned the floor and threw the towels into the washer. He made a pot of coffee and poured himself a mug. He glanced over at the book. He was certain without knowing it for a fact that it had something to do with what had transpired. It was only after delving into it that she had become ill. That did not explain her being outside in the rain in the dark or where she was going. Thank God for Shamus who had not let go of her. His head ached. He took three aspirin to ease it. He was at a total loss. I am just an ordinary guy he thought. I am not a superhero. I am not a ghost tracker and I have not one clue what I am going to do. He looked over at the journal again. Damn it. He picked it up and went down the hall. He sat on the rug outside her door and began to read.

September 21, 1929 –

It has been one week. Emma still will not obey. She has been in the attic every day despite my telling her it was off limits. Oh Evelyn, my love what has her so preoccupied there that she would risk my anger. I have had to take away her toys but she is undaunted by it. She is not the girl we knew.

September 23, 1929 –

In a panic I searched for Emma. She was supposed to be in the barn but no sign of her. As I turned I saw a reflection of something that caught my eye. It was in the window of the attic looking down at me. I am certain I did not imagine it. In my fright I thought of the child and raced to the stairs and up them. She was sitting on the floor with that doll. I called to her but she ignored me. I called to her again and got the same. It was then I ordered her to get up. Oh Evelyn, she has your sickness. Our child turned to me in a voice not of her own but that of a bone chilling guttural tone of an old man and she screamed at me. "No!" I slapped her dearest, I could not think. All I could hear is that voice. Our Emma began to cry then and I took her from that room and had it padlocked. It seems to be the cause of all of her troubles.

September 26 1929-

The nightmares have begun as of these past two nights. I do not know what to do or how to soothe them. She is afraid that he will be angry with her now that she can no longer enter the attic. She pleads with me Evelyn to allow her. The doctor will be here in the morning. She appears to be suffering from delusions. There is no he but I cannot make her see that. She only cries and says I do not understand how angry he will be. I am afraid our Emma will need to go away. I cannot let that happen. I must find it in me to help her. Help me, Evelyn I am so lost.

Jake looked over to the bed. Ally was breathing evenly. He went on to the next entry engrossed in its words.

September 27, 1929 –

The doctor has diagnosed her with delayed grief of your passing my love. He said it is not uncommon for it to take time to develop but he sees no need to usher her away to an asylum. With time and care she will come through this and be the happy child she once was. I can only pray that he is correct in his judgements. When I made note of the sound that emanated from her I was told it was part of her acting out. I am uncertain but the attic will remain locked just to be safe. I wonder should I take her from here on a trip. To the ocean perhaps. I can spare time soon. Do you remember Evelyn how she loved that week in New Jersey?

September 29. 1929 –

I have halted her studies. Her character has become more concerning and I do not trust her leaving this house. Mrs. Frank avoids her. I think she frightens her with her odd ways. I shall bring a tutor in no matter the cost so she does not fall adrift in her education. I know not what else to do.

October 1, 1929 –

We found Emma outside last eve. I am growing more worried by the day. What has happened to our dear girl? She is a stranger to me. Her nightdress torn and soaked with dew from the grass. Where had she been? In the woods? At the river? Her only excuse was that he was waiting for her. Who was he? Her imaginary friend? That was not possible! Where was he waiting? I am beginning to grow thin on patience. I may have to have another physician see her. I cannot depend on the town quack to be correct. If he was wrong our precious daughter is in peril.

Jake felt the hair at the back of his neck stand up when he finished that entry. Was she going to Emma? Was George Henry out there waiting? Was that who Shamus had picked up on? It would explain his actions. He was defending her but from what? From who? Was Ally in the midst of a nervous breakdown? Was Emma? He was as clueless as Sebastian.

October 9, 1929 -

Our sweet, sweet Emma is spiraling Evelyn. The doctor has suggested she be admitted. Her delusions are becoming violent in nature. She spit at me tonight when I called to her. She accused and said it was my fault that he is angry. Very angry. I have no other choice but to let them care for her where she will not be a danger to herself. I do not know dearest Evelyn what she may do next. In less than a week's time I will take our child that I vowed to protect with my life at your dying request and hand her off to others more capable than I. Forgive me my love. I do not know any other solution.

Jake turned the page. It had watermarks that had bled into the ink making it difficult to read. In a moment he realized that it was tears that stained it. Sebastian's tears.

October 14, 1929 –

They found after hours of searching our sweet, precious Emma at the edge of the river face down in the water. They believe she fell from the rocks above at the trestle. Oh Evelyn, our baby is gone. I am amassed with grief. Our Emma has drowned. How do I go on without her? She was the light within me. She was the light within you. I have failed as a father. I have failed our sweet child and will suffer the rest of my days for my ignorance. I shall mourn her loss until I leave this earth. Evelyn I am sorry. Emma please forgive me.

That was the final entry. He was full of sadness for Sebastian, for Emma. As he rose he groaned. His legs had gone numb from sitting like that. He stumbled and recovered but dropped the journal. As he picked it up a small piece of aged paper fluttered to the floor. As he read the contents he was a statue.

My daddy does not believe me. He thinks that George Henry is made up. He will not unlock the attic. He will not even as I beg him that he is waiting and will be angry. He wants to play and I cannot go there. It is forbidden. I am afraid. He is very, very angry. I must find a way.

The cry of a helpless little girl. Jake had he of had one shred of doubt before was completely convinced. George Henry had lured her to that river. He glanced over at Ally. This could not wait and he could only pray she would be strong enough to take this news.

CHAPTER TWELVE

Ally

Why was Jake waking her? She was so tired. "I'm sorry," he told her "but you need to see this. He held out the paper to her. "You need to finish the journal. Tonight." By half past five she was done and closed the book. Her eyes were full of tears. He felt like crying with her. "Jake, Oh Jake...he" "Yes Ally I know." He held her until the alarm went off at eight. He shut it off and studied her sleeping figure. She had scared him badly last night. He was afraid for her. For her state of mind. Now she would never accept that George Henry was not coming. He was helpless to help her.

"I do not know why I was out there," she replied as he asked her again when she woke. "Honestly." He believed her. She was out of it. "How do you feel?" Ally told him she was no longer feeling ill and actually was hungry. Jake smiled softly at her. That was a good sign wasn't it? Over toast and scrambled eggs he recounted how he had awaken to Shamus and how he had found her wandering towards the small patch of woods. He did not mention the dog's actions. She was already living in fear of what could not be anything less than demonic. "I am so sorry. I have made your life hell. That never was my intention." "I know that Ally. This is neither our baggage. We have both been catapulted into another dimension where reasoning and logic do not exist." After taking Shamus out for a long overdue walk he suggested they do something today. Something fun. If that could still be found.

As they rolled around the rink Jake saw the tension seep from her. She was enjoying it. The low lights. The multi colored ball sending brilliant dots slowly twirling into the air. The sights and sounds of thirty some other skaters. The smell of the popcorn. She was relaxing. How desperately he needed her to do so. He was worn thin from trying to anticipate every minute, every second. Ally felt good inside for the first time in days. She was grateful Jake had the presence of mind to get her involved with something other than ghosts and attics. Her mind was still reeling from Sebastian's entries. From Emma's writing. She needed this distraction. She felt as though she were the one losing her mind lately.

Jake was so good. He never complained. He never blamed her for what she unsuspectingly had laid on him. His every thought was for her welfare. She gave him a quick smile, a real smile Jake noticed as she passed him on the floor. It was good to see her like this. She was the Ally he met that first day. She had fought off the ramblings in her head and was letting herself have a good day. An average, normal, no cares at all day. He had to admire her for it. He knew she was a total mess inside. He had an idea. In the hopes of keeping this day on a high note he asked if she would like to get lunch at the restaurant. "I would really like that. It's been a bit." She liked going to Josie's. The place was a haven despite some of people who frequented it. No one besides that awful Clara Finley had said anything to her. They were indifferent or polite. She took either as a win.

"Let me guess, Club?" She chose the Ham and Swiss. While they ate Jake asked if she would be okay with hanging out here for an hour or two while he went to another site he had going. It had been weeks and the land owner was going to expect results. "I need to see what is left to do and get with Mike." She understood. He had put his entire life on standby. It wasn't fair. She did not like the position she had him in. It made her guilty and sad. Of course she would stay as long as he needed her to. "Do you think Hamilton's has needles?" "Needles?" "What for and yeah, he has everything and then some." "I tore my favorite shirt on a tree branch the other day." Hmmm. When was that? She smiled at him again. She hadn't been out of his sight...that he knew of. Was she becoming more practiced in her disappearing that she could now move about undetected? He looked at his watch. "Do you need money?" Ally replied she did not but thank you. He kissed her forehead, gave Josie a wave and drove away. Ally waited long enough for Josie to sit with her and after a few moments she said she was going to see Mitchell. Josie gave her a small hug. Poor thing. Jake had been keeping her apprised and things did not seem well at all for her.

"Is there an access road to the trestle?" Mitchell turned to her. "Yes but why?" "I have been wanting to see it. It does border my land you know." True but considering why would she want to? The road would be better than the woods he figured. The tracks would be a cinch save for the nearer you came to the bridge the more open the planks were. One could get their foot through it. "I am going either way I just wanted to know if there indeed was a road."

Mitchell could go with her. He could close up for a time. He had seen Jake leave. Ally had come with him and had no transportation. She would have to walk the highway. "No," she told him "I appreciate the offer but it is a nice day and I can make it on my own." "Exercise and fresh air will do me good." He relented. He couldn't exactly force his company on her.

The job had taken longer than he planned. He was glad she was with his aunt. At least he didn't have to worry about her and had gotten some things done. She would be fine with the extended stay. She was a good sport. "She said she was going to Hamilton's" "When was that?" "She was here for a bit so maybe hour? Hour and a half ago?" Was it longer? She had been pretty busy. It was conceivable that she really wasn't sure. Jake sighed heavily. So much for an ordinary day. He kissed Josie and said they would see her soon.

He sat down next to her on one of the huge boulders that lined either side of the creek. Above them were massive cement lengthwise pilings that jutted out a few feet from the wooden trestle stabilizing the ties and tracks themselves. He looked at the water below. From this height he guessed it to be a good twenty feet beneath them. "Why Ally?" "Did Mitchell tell you?" "I just knew." "I had to

Jake." "I had to see if I could feel Emma
here." "I get it Ally," Jake told her softly,
"but the idea of you down here alone bothers
me. After last night..." He didn't have to
say it. He was afraid for her. Suddenly she
regretted her impulse. She should have waited.
He had enough on his mind. "I would have
brought you." She knew that. Why hadn't she
just waited? The last thing she wanted to do
was alienate him. He was her rock and she
would not have made it this far without his
persistent care of her. "I think she
fell...looking for him or seeing and it
frightened her." Jake agreed. It was highly
probable that Emma had never seen his true self
back then. She had befriended him. She was
not afraid of him.

They spent the rest of the afternoon until
just before the sun went down on the boulder.
Jake only hoped that the journal and the river
today would bring her some small closure.
Knowledge is as powerful as a weapon. He
further hoped and prayed to be honest that
having more pieces to this tragedy would ease
her mind somewhat. She, he had an ominous gut
feeling, was going to need every ounce of self-
preservation that was in her. On the way home
Jake stopped to get the Fish Dinner for two and
a side of stew for Shamus. He owed that dog

her life. He would not be convinced of less. Home. He pulled in. What a difference a day makes. He was not overjoyed to be there as normally he would be. Too many questions. Too many reminders that it was no longer his get away from it all place.

As he watched her fork the flaky filet into her mouth he had a wild thought. Should he keep record as Sebastian had? Just in case? In case of what he asked himself? In case Ally spiraled as Emma had? She was already on her way. They played a game of cards to wind up the evening. He knew he was going to have to leave her again over the next few days. He couldn't ask Josie to keep taking time away from the restaurant. It posed a dilemma but he would figure it out. Another addition to the growing to do list. When they were saying goodnight Jake asked her to sleep in the loft with him. She was receptive to it thankfully. If he had her up there she would not be able to get past him and the stairs without him knowing. Shamus would sleep at the bottom rung. He patted the dog and told him in a whisper. "No shenanigans tonight boy." The dog looked at him. He knew.

The next two days were heavenly. No ghosts, no night time adventures. Maybe knowledge was that powerful. He would be seeing Mike in the morning. What to do about Ally? Things were better but he wasn't going to push that envelope. He dialed Josie. Would Ally serve as extra help? His aunt was more than appreciative to have her and would keep her eye on her as well. Now to sell it to Ally. "I waitressed back in college as a second job to make ends meet. I would be able to do it." That was easy. He would take it. Not much came simple these days. He had a good week's worth of work to finish. Not having to worry about her would make it a lot smoother on him. That lasted four days. On the fifth morning Jake awakened to find her sitting up in bed an angry scowl on her pretty features. When he asked what was wrong she turned to face him and yelled at him in a sinister burly tone. "Nothing is wrong! Stop watching me! You are always watching me." "Can you not ever just leave me be?" He recoiled. Whoa! What the hell was that all about? That wasn't like her.

He called Mike. They only had a half day left. Could he manage it? Mike said it would not be a problem and he would let him know when it was completed. He rang Josie. She was sorry to hear Ally was not herself and said she would miss her. The morning was spent in thought. Ally was re- reading the journal on the living room floor, her earlier outburst forgotten. If she even knew she had one. Jake, however, saw it for what it was. The beginning of the end. She opted for her own bed around nine. He regarded her carefully. Her mood had improved but he was taking no chances. Once she was asleep he threw a quilt down in the entrance and set the pillows against the jam. He would camp out here every night if he had to. She was not pulling another vanishing act. The nightmare started shortly afterwards. "I won't let you take her." Emma's child-like voice. "Ally don't let him trick you." "He is a bad man." Ally's low voice. "I am too weak to stop him Emma." Emma crying. "Please Ally. Fight him." High shrill laughter that belonged to neither. To an insane being. That was the only way he could describe it but it was coming from Ally. "I hear you," Jake said crossing himself. Shamus whimpered. "It's okay boy." The dog looked at him a moment and then lay his head back down. Two minutes after that he and Jake were both on their feet. Shamus was snarling, his ears at full alert. He jumped up on the bed staring out the window. It was only then that Ally screamed and sat up.

He had her in his arms. She remembered this one. Their voices anyhow. He was not going to say that they had come from her. "It was so real," she whispered. "I heard her." "I heard him laugh." She did not mention any odor. She did not have to. It lingered in the room. Jake coughed. It was pungent. Ally did not seem to notice. Why? All control had been vanquished. Now he was here. Jake knew it. He apologized for the lateness of the hour but Father James accepted the call without hesitating. "I have not been given the permission that would sanction an exorcism," he apologized. "I was going to call you tomorrow." Jake told him of what he had just witnessed and of the smell. The priest sent up a silent prayer. "To be truthful," Jake replied, "I'm not sure it would even help." "Father I don't think he is trying to take her over. I think he is trying to lure her to her own demise." "Where is she now?" He looked over at her where she slept on the bed beside him in the loft. He had to get away from that smell. "I have her with me." "It is in the dreams that his power grows. I think you should have her take sleeping pills. They will make her dream less." Jake chewed that over. "If that does not work we will house her here until we can resolve this." He hung up grateful once again to him for the advice and the offer but wasn't at all sure if either suggestion would be good right now. He put his arm around her as he drifted off. He wasn't sure of anything except that he would do whatever it took to keep her safe.

CHAPTER THIRTEEN

Mrs. Frank's Daughter

Mid-September. No closer to answers than two months ago. Jake was closer, though, to his own breaking point. Think! He slowly went back through Sebastian's writings. Ally was sound asleep beside him. She slept too much but in these times it allowed Jake to collect his own scattered thoughts. The housekeeper was the only known other in that house. He estimated her to be at least fifteen years older than her employer. He used that she was married to base it on. She would be well over a hundred and deceased as well. Did she have children? If so had she spoken to them of her time there? More questions.

A U.S. Census Poll brought up the name Bertha Frank 1940. Summit County Maryland. Her age listed as forty-four. The only other names in the household were Robert Frank and Jane Frank. Below the margin but counted. They were toddlers. He was sure of it. His next searches were for them. Robert Frank, deceased

1989. Jane Frank 71. Fort Lauderdale, Florida. Could it be? It had to be. A lead. Finally. Over breakfast he posed the situation to Ally. "Let's go away. Florida." Why would he want to go anywhere? She couldn't even remember which day was which lately. Fun in the sun? No, that wasn't it. Jake recognized her confusion. "Ally, I found Mrs. Franks daughter." Her eyes went to his. "I mean I believe it is her. I want to know."

"I'm afraid to go. I want to know but what if..." What would one more what if matter? "I know you are but I have two purposes for going. She is the only living person we know of that is even remotely connected to that time. We have to see if she knows anything...anything at all. I'm grasping at straws here and I realize that but it is better than just sitting on our thumbs." He did not want to say his other reason but there was no way around it. She had to know. "Ally," he began in a serious but quiet tone. "We don't talk much about this. We worry. We search our brains but between us there has not been a lot of discussion."

"I need you to know that I can't take much more of this. "I don't want to hurt your feelings but I have to be away from here." You need to recharge...I need to recharge. I have nothing left. I cannot think. I am mentally exhausted. I am worn thin from gauging every minute. Every second. Worried that I may overlook some small detail for which there will be consequences. Drained from trying to stay one step ahead of what will or will not happen." Now he made her cry. It was not his intention but it had to be said. He couldn't be more truthful than that.

Josie was more than happy to keep Shamus. She wished them well sending up a prayer for them to find some peace while they were gone. The flight was only a bit over two hours but it was long enough for them to put a plan together. They could not just show up at her doorstep and ask her about her family business. He was not even sure she would see them. It was decided to call and ask for a meeting with her. As the attendant did last call for drinks he wondered if being as far away from Edgerton as they could get would make a difference. Did ghosts have GPS?

They checked into their hotel. She walked out through the sliding glass window to their first floor patio. Jake had booked oceanfront. It was so warm. How lovely to be able to look out and see the beach. The water. He joined her there slipping his arms around her. "The sunset is going to be beautiful." He smiled. "Ally, whether we find out anything or not, can we just try to enjoy being here?" She thought of what he had said to her last night. They both needed this break. She nodded. "I will try." That is all he could ask of her.

He put in the call to the number listed for J. Frank. A young woman's voice picked up on the other end. Jake introduced himself and inquired if he could speak to Jane Frank. When asked what it pertained to he paused. "It is of a personal nature." She told him her name was Missy Jones and that she was Miss Frank's assistant slash secretary and that she was out and not expected back until late. He could leave his number and she would get back to him the following day. It would have to do.

They dined at the hotel restaurant. Jake ordered the shrimp pasta. Ally the blackened Tuna. Jake asked for the wine list and added a bottle of Merlot. He led the conversation. He was not going to let her withdraw. Not here. In a few moments she was more relaxed and even laughed at one of his awful attempts at a joke. It was terrific not to have the next sentence be about what they were fleeing from. "The sun will be going down soon." "Let's watch it together." He ordered another bottle of wine to be sent to their room and paid the tab. Jake lowered himself onto one of the chaise loungers and pulled her back against him wrapping his arms around her again. It was amazing. The reds, pinks and golds all melting together in the horizon. It was hard to tell where it ended and the water started. Between the effects of the wine and the lull of the ocean she slept soundly. They awoke to brilliant sunrise. Jake succeeded in talking her into an early morning swim. Her good mood had continued over and he was not taking one moment for granted. They showered and ordered room service. The hours passed and by noon he was antsy. Was she going to reach out to him? Had the message even been given? It was then his cell rang. He picked it up and nodded to Ally. It was her. He introduced himself and excused the intrusion on her time.

What was he going to say? She asked what his reason for calling was. "I'm not sure how this is going to sound but myself and my girlfriend Allison Mcdonald"...he glanced at Ally who was rolling her eyes. He grinned..."well we wanted to speak to you about your mother and her employment with Sebastian Morley. If you can recall." "That is not a name I ever expected to hear again in my lifetime young man," she replied. He was hopeful. "I shall see you. If you and your lady can come to me at my country club at four today I will meet with you after my tennis match." Jake said they would be there. She gave him the name and the address. "Come to the clubhouse. Give them my name and they will see you in." As he hung up he couldn't suppress the elation he was feeling. At last. Maybe this would bring answers.

Jane Frank was small but wiry with an athletic build. Her grey hair was fashionably styled. She still wore her tennis shorts and matching shirt. She was a pinnacle of social grace and standing. As they sat he wondered how to begin but he needn't have bothered. She delved right in. "How would one of your perspective ages know anything of Sebastian Morley?" Jake and Ally exchanged glances. She was going to think they were crazy. He explained that Ally was related distantly and had inherited the home. He told her of the journal and that her mother had been mentioned in several of the entries. Had she ever spoken of it?

Jane Frank took a sip of her lemonade. Yes, she had many times, especially in her later years. "She would say that Sebastian had gone insane after the death of his child." That much they knew. "My parents came to America from England not so many years before she started working for him. She had never had the responsibility of a child before then and it would be part of her duties." "The child, she said, suffered from mental illness but it wasn't until it was too late she discovered that. She needed the job and had done the best she could with her. She talked to people that were not there. Her behavior was troubling." They knew that also. "That is all I know in relation to her job assignment." It would be as it was with Silas. More background. "Thank you, we appreciate you taking time out of your day for us." Jane Frank looked Ally in the eyes. "Young lady," she said, "Do you not want to hear the rest?" Ally quickly apologized. They were all ears. Jane Frank smiled. She sure was spry in mind. "It is not so much what I remember about what happened before the poor girl's drowning. It is more about what Sebastian did after."

Jake and Ally listened intently without cutting in. This is what they had traveled so far to hear. They were sure of it. They were interrupted by Missy Jones who appeared at their table. "Your five pm call car will be in the valet Miss Frank. Is there anything else?" "I would like you to meet my new friends." She winked at them. "Tell Manford I will be outside...when I am outside." Ally giggled. She was cute as a button with the barb. Missy Jones laughed. "She's something isn't she? Without a doubt. This was one interesting woman. "You are okay until then?" "Yes dear.

I am quite aright. Goodnight." She addressed them as her assistant retreated. "She is a mother hen." The three of them shared a moment of laughter.

"As I was about to tell you Sebastian Morley was beyond grief stricken as you may imagine. Emma was his pride and joy. She was all he had left of his wife. She is the light within me. She is the light within you...He clearly even as nearly a child himself had given his all to her. It may have been, Jake thought, his way of carrying on his love for Evelyn. "The man could not even bring himself to inter her to the cemetery." What did that mean?

"In those days, you understand, cremation was not a widely used or popular concept save for possibly infectious diseases. What? He had her cremated? "In later life my mother was haunted by that. He had her ashes put into the fireplace where he would sit each night and stare into the flames." Jake was dumfounded. Ally was horrified. Jane Frank went on. "I believe that was the reason she left that house shortly after and moved half way across the country to be free of it. Her guilt of knowing and being a party to it was too much for her," she concluded. "I'm sorry but I do not know of anything else I can tell you but this has been a most pleasurable day for me despite the tragedy of it all. It isn't often one gets to retrace a century and walk in the footprints of their passing."

Later as they walked the water's edge hand in hand letting the waves wash over them they talked over what Jane Frank had said. "That is lunacy," Jake expelled still trying to grasp what led Sebastian down that road. "Why would he put her there? Now I see why the burial place was reported as undisclosed." "Was he so filled with sorrow that he had to keep her near? Is that why the book was there? Had he found Emma's letter and put it and the journal to rest with her?" He wasn't sure what Ally's response was going to be but he was not prepared for it. Very quietly. "He believed that he was destroying her demons with fire. He wanted her soul to go on without them." Jake looked into her eyes. It wasn't her summation. He knew it had come from Sebastian. He knew it was correct and he knew that Ally had done it again.

They spent another two days in the sun. No nightmares. No disturbances. Falling off to the lull of the ocean at night, the long walks, just being here had made the difference in both of them. Jake emerged from the tide and shook himself of the drops of water that beaded on his skin. I am just like my dog. He laughed out loud. Florida had been the right decision. While they had not learned a lot more any small thing was another piece. It was more the significant change in both of them. Ally was calm. She was having the best of days in a long while. As for himself Jake was revived. He was strong. He had needed this. The only downfall is that they would have to go back to where it all waited for them. It was too much too hope for he sighed as he finished drying off that leaving had somehow miraculously severed the chain that bound them.

CHAPTER FOURTEEN

Spiraling

Good things do not last. They had only been home two days. "Ally, ALLY wake up!" She was screaming uncontrollably. He had to drag Shamus down the steps. "STAY!" He held her as she sobbed. This one began the downward trend for her. She was silent. She was a mass of tears. She was kind. She was mean. She was hot. She was cold. Jake couldn't keep ahead of her next mood and as the sun went down each night he would find himself on the brink waiting for the nightmares which were there to stay

She had gone down the hall around nine with the Rottweiler at her heels. She did not want to sleep in the loft nor on the couch. He could not persuade her. It was a source of contention for him but he could not demand or force her to. So he waited alone. He must have dozed off. It was twelve thirty. Shamus was snarling viciously, gnashing his teeth as he repeatedly hurled himself at the closed door. Why was it locked? "OPEN THE DOOR ALLY OR

I WILL BREAK IT DOWN!" Nothing. Silence but for the dog who was going berserk. He kicked it in and was nearly trampled by Shamus who lunged into the air landing on top of Ally as he continued his attack against an unseen foe. The stench was sickening. She was just sitting there. Eyes glazed over unaware of the dog who was in full defense mode. Unaware of the door. Unaware of Jake. He drug her by the shirt down the hall and deposited her in an arm chair. He had to get her out of there. His anger was instant. "WHAT THE HELL WERE YOU DOING? WHAT WERE YOU TRYING TO PROVE?" That jolted her out of her trance. Had she purposely planned this? Had she deliberately shut Shamus out? She had to of. He would not have left on his own. "I had to Jake." "Why Ally, WHY??" "He told me to."

It took forever to get the dog under control. It took forever to get Ally to fully come around. He told her to? That was it! He would make sure she would not be going in there again. He stretched out in the chair, Ally and Shamus finally sleeping as he kept watch. He would do whatever he had to. He would no longer take a passive back seat. The next three nights were worse than the one before it. The nightmares were full scale terrifying as were her screams. She was unaware each time. By day she would be listless. Lethargy was overtaking her. By night she would be in his clutches. Jake reached his limit. She had not argued against him when told she would no longer be sleeping by herself nor go into the room. He gave her the choice of the sofa or his bed with or without him in it. Thankfully she chose the latter. He went as far as to bring her belongings out before he snapped the padlock into place after repairing the door. He realized he was following old footsteps but he was out of options and patience. "Coward! Why don't you pick on someone your own size," he screamed.

It was the 19th of September when Jake opened his own book. Ally was sound asleep. That is all she was capable of lately. Sleep from exhaustion. Sleep from depression. Become prey in doing so. Father James's voice. "It is the dreams that make him stronger...He hated what he was about to do but nothing would stay his hand. She was the woman he loved. She was a human being. She was not a science experiment but he would do so nonetheless.

September 19, 2011 –

Forgive me Ally for embarking on this betrayal but I do know not what else to do.

Jake, pen in hand, heard the overwrought voice. He knew that same sense of hopelessness. He held the journal he now would keep. History had come home to roost.

The very next morning Jake quietly told her he was going to have to take her to be seen. That set her off. First she yelled in a tone that did not belong to her, then flat out said no and then she began to beg as she cried. "Please Jake, please don't make me do that." "I am afraid." He felt like a louse as her pleas became more desperate. I'm sorry Ally but I am afraid...not to." "Please, thy will think..." "I know." He already was thinking it himself. He gave in. She was close to the edge now. He wouldn't push her over. For what seemed like the hundredth time he held her until her tears stopped. "You cannot have her you piece of twisted garbage. You will not win."

In return for Jake's temporary reprieve Ally had to swear to eat. Swear to start walking with him and Shamus again and swear to fight harder than she had fought for anything. Ever. "I need you Ally," he said softly. "I cannot do this on my own."

September 21, 2011 –

I thought I had found the weak link. The walk, the food, the fight to stay awake. To stay aware. All in vain for it made not one difference. She is trying. I know she is trying.

Ally began to stir. He put down the pen. He waited. His next entry was a live show and needed no words. "No, NO Emma you can't leave me." A ten year old Emma. "I have to Ally. It is my time. Ally crying. "It is not safe. It is a trick. Take my hand Emma." "Goodbye Ally." Louder now. Imploring, beseeching on your knees begging..."Come back." Crying harder..."Why? Why Emma?" The very words he had asked of her. "George Henry has a new playmate." He shook her lightly. "C'mon Ally. C'mon you can do this. Wake up." "She's gone Jake. Emma is gone." It hurt him to have to say to her..."I know." It hurt him even more to know that she was on borrowed time.

September 23, 2011 -

Emma is not coming back. Ally is despondent. She has stopped eating. She is so pale. She stopped trying. Leaving had not helped. I regret ever returning. It made a situation no one could imagine unless have walked their path far worse. Punishment? I do not know. I am humbled. I have found what I cannot do anything about.

September 27, 2011 –

He has been here three days now. Each visit weakening her more. I forced her to eat these past days. She managed a bite here and there. Shamus paces. He is nervous. We are all nervous.

September 29, 2011 –

She has to go in. I cannot do this. Drugs? Hypnos-therapy to erase him? Is that possible? She will never forgive me. I have tried to get her to see that Emma being gone is a good thing. She is free. She is safe. Isn't that what this has been about? Where it all started? My own pen denies the truth. Ally is her replacement. What does he want? Her sanity? Her life? I cannot care for her. I am not able...He had become Sebastian. His pain had become Jake's own. To slowly go crazy while you watch someone you love go insane.

October 3, 2011 –

Bloodcurdling laughter. Cries in the night. My dog. Her dog at constant vigil. I cannot recall when I last left her side. She battles him and fails. She loathes herself for what this is doing to me.

I do not want to let her go.

I will not let her go

I do not want her give in and let go of me.

CHAPTER FIFTEEN

The Anniversary

October 4, 2011 –

I am in a severe predicament. If I take her they will not look past her state of mind. They will not look past all I see every day. It takes all of my thoughts, all of my energy to keep him at bay. I cannot protect her there. She will be helpless.

Jake lay back against the pillows. Ally was breathing evenly beside him. Dreamless slumber. For now. Would that last? He had reached his last mile. There had to be a way out. Had Florida been a fluke. Could they leave now? Could he risk it? He was stronger now. Ally opened her eyes. A barely audible, "he will follow me." She heard him. She heard his silent words again. She was still in there. He wrapped her in his arms and kissed her hair. Find the way he asked of himself as closed his eyes. What are you missing damn it? He went back to the beginning. Where was the answer?

What was his end game? Mrs. Frank. Sebastian. Jane Frank. Silas. They in their own way had brought pieces that were laying on the table. How did they all fit together? He needed to go over every word said. Every entry written. There had to be a connection. A clue. He eased himself away from her and reached into the bedside table for Sebastian Morley's journal. He glanced over at his own stopping him in mid-motion. The same desperation. The same dark abyss. The dates. Jake you dumbass...the dates. That was his end game. Emma's anniversary. He slept. He had one answer and ten days to figure out the rest.

He let her sleep until eight. "Wake up." "What is wrong Jake is something wrong?" He studied her. She was too thin. Her beautiful eyes held only fear now. Please don't let me be wrong. "I know what he wants." "I know how he works." "Tell me please." "If you will try to eat I promise...I will." It wasn't much but she ate some of the toast. She promised she would try soup later. It was all he could ask of her. "Can you make a walk?" He carried her the rest of the way. She was but a feather these days. He helped her onto the log. Shamus put his head in her lap. In the quiet of the clearing he began.

"Evelyn Morley had the tendencies but he hadn't the time to devour her. Childbirth took her instead. I believe that is how he got to Emma. Sebastian was right. Emma was mentally ill Ally." She listened as he held her close. He preyed on that from the second it reared its ugliness. She was an innocent child already bearing a cross. She must have been so lonely not understanding what was happening to her. George Henry understood. He pretended to be her friend. He could move back and forth between her and himself." He paused to look at her, "the way he does with you Ally." "He could bend her to his maniacal will." "Jake?" "It's George Henry who was insane. In a soulless death sentenced to eternal damnation he craves company."

It was growing cooler. He had to get her back inside. She was too weak to fight off even the slightest cold. "I can make it," "Are you sure Ally, I will carry you again." She did it. They had to stop several times and allow her to rest but she did it. She ate part of the soup. He was encouraged. "Can you stay awake?" There was still so much left to say. She nodded. "I think so." More encouragement. I have to be right. No mistakes. "I don't know how it is going to all play out yet...but

I will." She gave him a small smile. He had gotten her this far.

"There is still a lot I don't know but I think Emma was a vessel." "He recognized it. If he had her she would take him to others and all he had to do is sit back, watch, choose and wait." "Why me?" Her eyes were sad. "I have no such afflictions. There is no association." Jake took her hand. "He didn't need one with you. He had a built in hole card. You are Emma's cousin." She took that in. No that wasn't right. Had Jake forgotten? He must have. Sebastian Morley was her mother's uncle. Emma was Evelyn's daughter.

"Evil has no logic Ally," he explained. "When she called out to you. When she tried to break away he found his way in. The vessel." "I'm tired Jake." He picked her up and carried her to his bed. Shamus licked her hand on his way up. He laid beside her and cradled her. We can talk more in the morning. "Jake?" "Yes?" "How do you know any of this?" He took her hand again. "I cannot tell you. I'm not sure myself." "Go to sleep. We are right here." "Go to hell you son of a whore," he whispered. "I'm coming for you now." Jake closed his own eyes. He was ready.

She ate a few bites. She walked with him a short distance and he carried her the rest of the way. Ally bent giving Shamus a kiss on his wet nose. She could not have a better companion. He sensed her every need. He would give his life for her. "I love you." The dog regarded her. He licked her face. He knew. Jake watched them. They were his world. "I have more to tell you." In the comfort of their bed he opened more doors. How he knew he did not care. "We have to make it through the fourteenth, I just know that." "It completes the cycle." "What cycle?" "Ally, what I have told to you so far...it's right." Before she could ask how he was so certain he continued. "I know it is. It is the same way...he looked into her eyes..."you answer what I have not asked you." "I don't know where it comes from." "I know." "I think you have the gift of discernment." "Psychic?" Ally yawned. "Do you need to sleep? "I don't want to just yet." Good. He needed to keep her mind working. "I have to be honest. The rest of this is pure theory but just listen." She nodded and he gave her a gentle hug. "Jake?" "Yes?" "Where is he?"

He wished he knew. "Just listen. Please?" The last thing he wanted was for her to lose focus. He couldn't let that happen. "Just trust me Ally." She did. He would never harm her with outlandish ideas. "Not really. Not psychic but you do have an ability. I think that is dangerous to him." "Either that..." he did not want to say it. "Or...it makes you more interesting." She cowered and he pulled her back against him. "We cannot outrun him Ally. "We have to cheat him out of your soul." "That means and I hope the bastard is listening..." Ally's eyes grew wide with terror. "Please don't say that Jake. Please." He finished his sentence. He was done running. "You my beautiful woman, he told her in a gentle tone, "have to fight him." "But I've tried..." He cut her off. "Don't cry. It's okay. I know you tried." He did know. He could not fathom to have to be where she was. He was on the outside looking in. Ally was getting hit full blast. "This time...and do you remember the night I told you to never make me repeat life threatening matters?" She knew exactly what he meant. "This time you have to square off and spit right in his face. You have to fight with every ounce of your being." "Your mind is strong Ally. He knows and that is why he has tortured you so much. He needs to break you." "You have to let him know he can't."

Could she? She had been through so much. "Do you want to finish this later?" He eyes welled with tears. "No." He wasn't sure. She didn't look so well. "If he comes for me tonight...I need to know everything." He brought her up dinner. Grilled cheese while letting Shamus out and refilling his dishes. The dog padded up the stairs behind him and went to Ally. She patted the bed. "C'mon boy." With her dog curled up next to her and she laying back with his hand covering hers Jake resumed the conversation.

"As I was telling you earlier. It's a hunch but a plausible one." "I called it a cycle because I think that when Emma brought you in and he saw her replacement that in some way it has to coincide with her anniversary." "Why did he let her go now?" Jake sighed. "Ally...he thinks he has already won." "Look where you have been...where you are now. This has taken so much out of you. You are...well I don't know any other way of saying this to you but you are...damaged. His mark is on you." She knew. Her mind was going. He thought of the padlocked door. "He has gotten you to do his bidding once. He can control you. He is not going to let you go easily." He did not add if at all.

CHAPTER SIXTEEN

Hide and Seek

It was the seventh of October. No sign of him. Ally was still sleeping too much. She still ate too little. She still lived in fear. He looked over at her where she lay on the sofa underneath a warm blanket. Was he going to wear her down enough to take her own life? Was he going to see her damned to an asylum where he could torment her until her last day? He believed he knew when but how...where? One week. One week to try to get Ally prepared for the fight of her lifetime. What of the anniversary didn't mean what he presumed and he had no plans to end this? Could she take much more?

Lying next to her with Shamus at their bedside Jake prayed for Ally. He had to be right. The stench permeated the room. Shamus was bristling. Growling, throwing himself into the air as he went on attack. High pitched, hysterical insane laughter as Ally sat up. Shamus halted immediately. He was confused Jake thought. He would not attack her. He wasn't sure what to do. He sensed danger but that unearthly sound was coming from her. He began to whimper loudly. Ally did not notice. She did not hear. He grabbed her harder than he intended but she was slack and lifeless. Her body began to shake violently. A seizure. "Oh God no! Ally!" "Ally!" White foam spittling from the corners of her mouth. Her eyes rolled back into her head showing only the white of them. It stopped as sudden as it started. The EMS arrived within minutes. He had to. He was not a doctor either.

Once she was hooked up to monitors and given medication the attending physician had a portable EEG brought it. Electrodes were attached to the tab sensors. The needles going up and down on the paper. He looked at Jake his eyes narrowing and gestured for him to follow him into the hall to a private area. He wasted not one second. "I want to know what is happening to this girl." "Seizures can be caused by genetics, fevers...his tone became firm, accusing as he added "severe stress." "I am less concerned with the episode, it is her general appearance I want answers to." "Her eyes are sunken, her pallor is grey and her skin is stretched tightly over her facial bones. I can see her ribs." He was angry now. She is damn near emaciated."

"You better start talking. If not it will be the State Police you are talking to in less than twenty minutes." Silence. What was he supposed to tell him? The truth? He and Ally would both be committed. This is all my fault. I should not have given in. Manic screams from the cubicle. Ally thrashing to rip the IVs from her arms. Security holding him back. A shot administered as a nurse and an orderly held her down trying to stop the blood. To stop her. A few seconds later she went limp. It was chaotic. Rushing to get the electrodes out. Rushing to clean her and get new ports in her. Bandaging the wounds. Yelling. Heart stopped. Defibrillator. CLEAR! Again. CLEAR! Ally's skeletal body flopping with each hit of the pads. A long needle thrust into her chest. Again. CLEAR!

Beep. Beep. In sinus rhythm. They wouldn't let him in. Wouldn't let him near her. Ally had literally died on that bed. Oh God Ally I'm so sorry. Tears falling down. I'm so sorry. Why did you force her to fight? Why did you have to challenge him? He had been wrestled into an anteroom and the door barred by two officers. The third addressed him. "This is a welfare case. Are you responsible for her care?" Jake could only nod. I'm so sorry Ally. "Sir?" Jake looked up from the chair they insisted on. "Do you know what neglect is? It's right there in that room!" "The doctor is a mandated reporter. He has filed charges against you." Jake was not listening. Let them do whatever the hell they want to me. Oh God Ally. "Mr. Madden?" "MR. MADDEN!"

Jake was handcuffed, escorted to the awaiting squad car, taken to the post, processed and given a phone call. Ally. Damn it I cannot leave her. Ally! Raw fear. His bail was astronomical. Mike arrived an hour later. His court date was in two weeks. Criminal negligence. Mike said not a word until he was done. "My God Jake, they think you did this to her!" "I know." "Ally can't be alone there. Mike I lost her tonight." He sent a prayer for her well-being. Please watch over her. He was openly crying. He and Tim had known him almost thirty years. This did not happen. Ever. "She's in bad shape Mike, I should have taken her for help long ago."

Mike Moore pulled into the drop off zone at the hospital. "I will be in once I park." "Thanks, Mike but you don't have to do this." "I will come by in the morning to cover the bail and..." Mike cut him off. "I don't care

about the money. You are good for it. This is
me...covering your ass because I know if they
don't let you in...another trip to the police
post is in your future tonight." He was
greeted by security. "I just want to talk to
the doctor." He was desperate. He looked
desperate. They led him to the emergency doors
and told him to wait there. After what seemed
like an eternity the doctor came out. He was
no more pleasant than earlier. "I need to know
how she is." "Why? Why now?" He was right.
He should have done something. "Mr. Madden,
this is a serious situation. Now will you give
me answers? For her sake."

"She is mentally ill." His heart sank. He
said it. He had to. His coat said Dr. Rainz.
Why did that matter? Why had he noticed? The
room was a blur. Mike was next to him. "We
need to talk," he said quietly. "Follow me."
"She is in critically serious condition." "If
her heart stops again..." He had nearly killed
her. His ignorance, his stupidity. "Please let
me see her. Please." "She is in a drug
induced coma." NO. NO. He was there waiting.
"She is too weak physically to withstand any
more stress of any kind. It was my only option
for now." "Two minutes, Mr. Madden." He took
her hand. Ally please forgive me.

Mike took him to pick up Shamus who was nervously pacing up and down the hall outside the padlocked door. He grabbed a few clothes and locked up. "Thanks for coming Mike," he said as he put the dog into the cab. "I didn't want to involve Josie." He nodded. "Any time Jake, you know that." "Come by in the morning. We will go to the bank." I will be out to the Strideway."   He rubbed Shamus's head and turned the key. Please be okay Ally. Please.

He was at the hospital by ten. Dr. Rainz saw him as he was coming out of the cubicle. The man looked like hell Rainz thought as he called him to the side. "Can I see her?" "Please?" "Not right now. We just inserted a feeding tube into her. Let them finish up." "Meanwhile I have to say some things you are not going to want to hear." "If she gets past this I am having her transferred over to the state hospital for observation." Panic. "I cannot let you do that." He regarded Jake momentarily. "You do not have a say in this." She is unable to make decisions for herself, her condition proves that. You are neither her guardian nor relative. I say and my decision stands."

He cried again when he was finally allowed in. "Dr. Rainz said quietly from behind him. "We will start bringing her out of it tomorrow.

She will be here until she is stable. Her condition is still critical." State hospital. The timeline. George Henry. He had sealed her fate. He was allowed to remain with her the rest of the day.

"Mr. Madden, she is asking for you." Jake jumped up. She was awake. He had been back since dawn waiting. The heart monitor. The numerous IVs. The feeding tube. The catheter. Her voice weak, barely a whisper. "I'm afraid." He pulled his chair as close as he could to her. She looked the worst he had ever seen her. What had he done to her? What caused those screams? "I know Ally." "I'm here." Another whisper or an attempt at one, "I don't feel well Jake." "Shh." His hand covering hers. Quietly. Gently. Tenderly. "Stay with me Ally." "I need you."

Two more days passed. Had he gone? Ally was no better. She was clinging to life by a hair. Dr. Rainz grew more concerned every hour that went by. She had lost another half-pound despite the tubes that pumped protein and vitamins into her. Her heart rate was low. Medications for that. In sleep it would race. More medications. No answers. Why was she not responding to treatment? She was so fragile. Josie was caring for his dog. He was not going anywhere. "Take out the feeding tube." Rainz swung around to face him. "Excuse me?" Jake looked up at him from his place at her bedside. "They are not working and...well...I can get her to eat." "Give her protein shakes. Vitamins orally. Soup. As crazy as it sounds...She will try for me."

The Twelfth of October. The Thirteenth of October. He had managed to get her to eat. Spoons full and sips but she was doing it. She still could not stand. Could not walk unassisted. It would take a long time Rainz told him heavily...if she made it...to come back from this. He needed Jake to know tomorrow is not promised for any of us. She was as fragile mentally as she was physically. Her waking hours were filled with fear. Where was he? Ironically, it was only while she slept now that she found peace. "Jake?" He leaned in to hear her. "He's coming." And just like that...he did. Her head jerked. Her eyes rolled. Her body shook. She came to screaming. She was heavily sedated again. Her tiny wrists were secured to the rails as were her stick legs. She now weighed eighty nine pounds.

This was no seizure. He didn't give a damn what Rainz said. He had to see her. Had to talk to her. He had been ushered out but that was hours ago. He was not permitted entrance to her cubicle. Why? He was losing his own mind. It was early evening before Dr. Rainz came to him. "She is stable and resting but she does not want to see you?"

What? Impossible. Something was very wrong. "I'm sorry." Jake wasn't even paying attention to him. Why would she not want to see him? He had to see her. "I have to do what is in her best interest Mr. Madden. I will not jeopardize her health further." He halted a moment and what he said next made Jake's blood turn cold. He was listening now. "She said to tell you she is sorry but...you are..."I am what? SAY IT!" "She said you are killing her and that there will be no more hiding." He started to say that the last part he didn't understand but Jake couldn't hear him anymore.

CHAPTER SEVENTEEN

Jigsaw Pieces

Nine days. It was now October twenty second. The anniversary had passed. Was the threshold closed? He still had not seen Ally but had begged for updates and received them. She was at one hundred and one pounds. How? He was told the tubes were reinserted. They were producing results. That made no sense. More than a pound a day? She had been transferred to the mental health ward yesterday and was managing to eat on her own somewhat. They would take that as a victory. He had at least been able to throw enough weight around to keep her out of the state facility. She was still mentally on pins and needles. She had had a few rough nights. "Just say it...she has been having nightmares." He knew damn well what a rough night consisted of. Instant dread. Instant need to be with her.

No cause for alarm? To be expected in her condition. Was he serious? Jake hung up. Shamus came to his side. "It's okay buddy."

Nothing was okay. He was still at the Strideway. He was not going back except to collect his belongings when he was ready. He lived and breathed Ally. Why wouldn't she see him? You know why he told himself. You know who was in control that day. He just didn't get why she had not come back by now and want to see him. He knew she was in terror. He knew her condition would cease to improve if they continued. As much as he did not want to face it he knew she would not withstand another heart attack. The damage was done. He didn't know how she was fighting still. "Keep fighting Ally. Please." Anti-psychotics. Nerve pills. They were useless. Didn't they see that? He had to find a way to see her. He hurt for what she was going through. Alone. He could hear her soft voice. "Jake...I'm afraid." Please Ally. I have to get to you.

He took a stool at the counter. "I don't know Josie," he sighed. She didn't understand it either. Why wouldn't Ally see her nephew? She loved him. They had been inseparable throughout this whole ordeal. Why now? When she needed him most. "What are you going to do?" "Not sure." He was thinking about his day in court. That had not been pleasant but thankfully Dr. Rainz had made an appearance and told the judge there were unusual and mitigating circumstances. He was free to go. Free to go where? The only place he wanted to be he couldn't get to while Ally was held prisoner by her own mind. "I don't have any idea." He finally said. "None at all."

He had been wrong about Emma's date of death. It had meant nothing. Now every day was like two. Waiting, praying he wouldn't hear the worst. He had been certain. Did this mean he would take her slowly until there was nothing left of her? Did it mean he would push her off of her next cliff? He petitioned for immediate guardianship but even the lawyer doubted he would get it considering. Even if he did it would be a lengthy process. The avenues were blocked.

The journals he now kept in his head adding to them each night. He did not need to write it down any longer. He was living them.

It's the twenty fifth of October. Ally continues to struggle. She has dropped seven pounds. The medications that should be keeping her moods steady were only taking the edge off. Bad dreams. If only they were just bad dreams. It made his heart sink each time he would hear "I'm sorry no. She still does not want to see you." In the dark with Shamus at his side he whispered, "Ally?" "Can you hear me?" "I'm here." Could she?

The next two days went by. Jake ate. He slept or tried to. He drank. He took care of his dog but every other second was devoted to Ally. How he could help her? What was going to happen next? How much longer could she hang on? That last thought filled him with un-nameable sorrow. She was by all accounts barely clinging to a limb. How was this all going to end? Every road led straight towards badly. No detours.

On the thirtieth he made the decision to try to live again. Ally would be his first and only real thought but he was going to force himself to go through the motions. What other choice did he have? So much for that. On Halloween he was literally dragged to Josie's for her annual Trick or Trick Extravaganza. "You cannot go on like this," Mike told him. Jake was going. One way or the other he was getting him out of his depression at least for one night. Jake took a draw of his coffee.

Under different circumstances this would have been a celebratory occasion for him. He loved hosting it with his aunt. Most of the town turned out with their kids and grandkids. They could come in have coffee, warm cider, it didn't matter. Pastries and doughnuts. Candy and caramel apples. They both looked forward to this every Halloween. Tonight, however, every smile he gave, every laugh he joined in on was conjured up to not ruin this for her. He went out to check on Shamus. The dog was snoring in his heated doghouse Josie had bought for him last year on his birthday. He would love to be curled up in there too. How he had changed since Ally was gone. He dog was sad. There was no other word to describe it. In the daytime he looked for her everywhere only to lay down and whine when he couldn't find her. "I know," he said to the sleeping dog. "I miss her too." If that were only the case he would be without her in a heartbeat. If she was just gone by her own will he could have taken that. If it meant she would be okay he would gladly walk away but it wasn't like that. No one could tell him it was.

When he went back inside he saw Tim Moore getting around quite well with his cane accompanied by Joann, one hobo, one pirate and one ballerina. He went over to him while the kids were off getting their loot. He shook hands with him. "It's great to see you vertical again." He meant it. Tim was a good guy. They went over to a corner table that had just been vacated by a spider and a pumpkin.

After assuring him he was on the mend and would be back to full mobility very soon he asked in a hushed tone if there had been any change in Ally? He did not need a reply. Jake's face was enough. "I'm sorry." "Thanks Tim. One second at a time."

His cell rang as he and Josie were cleaning the aftermath of the party. He picked up fearing the worst. "She has been sleepwalking Mr. Madden. Tonight she went into a rage when she woke. She was calling for you as we sedated her." He was told the only reason they were involving him is they worry that she may harm herself wandering around unaware. He was the closest she had to anyone and did he have any answers that may calm her? Jake put his cell back into his jacket pocket. He wished he did. He kissed his aunt when they were done and said after he took out the trash he was going to grab Shamus and go. Josie wouldn't hear of it. "Jake, honey, just let him upstairs. I will keep him for a few days. He can run around and you know I love having him." "Thanks." His dog didn't belong cooped up in that motel any more than he did.

Showered and exhausted he turned out the lamp and got into bed. She called out for him. He couldn't stop thinking of that. Had she heard him? Did he just want to think she had? He woke a few hours later. Why he was not sure. Had he been dreaming? He didn't know that either but something was there. Something he couldn't explain or remember. Jake lie awake until dawn. Was she sleeping and stable again? Was she in his clutches again? What did that bastard want? Dejected and defeated he knew that answer was not going to matter soon. Eighteen days trying to fight with little respite. Eighteen days of wasting away again. Eighteen days of terror. Alone. He couldn't stand it. There had to be something that could be done.

He placed a call to Dr. Rainz's office when it opened. "We were going to give you a courtesy call this morning," the receptionist told him. "The doctor wants to transfer her to a facility better equipped to handle her." "Does she have insurance that you know of? There is not a lot going on there." He knew exactly what she meant. Ally was a nutcase in her eyes. His tone was gruff as he replied that he had no idea and did that mean she would go to a less qualified clinic? No he was told. "Dr. Rainz is making arrangements for her to go to The Gregory Institute up in Rapid City." He had connections there. That was over a hundred miles away. God no. A couple miles was one thing. At least he knew she was out there and

she knew he was.   He believed with all he had
that somewhere Ally was still there and that
she knew he was waiting for her.

One week from today she would be going.   She
would get the care she so desperately needed.
In all fairness he knew Rainz was doing the
best he could.   He knew that helplessness.
Should he have been honest in the beginning?
Would that force them to get that there was
nothing medical that would help her in the end?
He had pleaded to be allowed a visit before
then but the receptionist said that would be
the doctors call and he would be notified if
so.   To Jake it was a whopping no.   There was
no way he would rescind that decision.   Her
initial evaluation was thirty days but two
things would happen before then.   Ally would
expire from weakness. Ally would be permanently
committed.   It was a bitter reality he had to
face.   Was one fate better than the other?   Not
in her present state.   Either would be the
final destination.

To his shock Rainz called him personally the
next afternoon.   He could see her but if she
made one sign that she did not want him there
he would have to leave and not return or be
made to leave.   He had never been so entwined
with a patient as he was this one.   He went
against her wishes praying that Jake being

there would make some difference. Any difference. He doubted it but it was a chance. She wasn't strong enough to take on any confrontations so he had to swear he would go at any hint. Diminished capacity had been his words. "Oh Ally. Please I beg you...do not send me away." He jerked around. Was his own mind playing tricks now? Something had just happened. What though? It gnawed away at him the rest of the day. By late evening after a visit with Shamus he still could not shake it. It stayed with him as he finally fell off anxious about seeing her tomorrow. He gave up a silent prayer. "Thank you."

He waited to be buzzed into the third floor unit. She was in her room. Before being able to go in he was reminded of the restrictions Rainz had put on him. She had not carried any of the weight. He could see it from the doorway. She lie on the bed. The blankets pulled up around her. They did little to hide that she was growing smaller. He gazed at her sleeping figure. She looked no better than the last time he had seen her. What had he done to her? He went to her careful not to make a sound as he quietly put the recliner next to her. He sat there with his hand over hers for what seemed like hours before she opened her eyes.

Almost unheard she whispered, "Where have you gone? Why did you leave me?" Those two sentences seemed to deplete her. "Ally," "I will never leave." He did not say that she had denied him. He did not tell her that it was her doing. He couldn't. She was not responsible. He hated himself. This was his fault. Directly or indirectly Jake believed it was on him. Could he live with that? In that moment Jake found the true meaning of what being humbled really was. She was still here. He was in complete awe of her. She was in there somewhere. She wasn't giving in. He watched her sleep. Gratefully she was resting. He knew the difference up close and personal. No one would believe the hell she had walked and was still walking in. He would not have believed it himself but sadly for Ally every second of it was true. The thought of losing her was something he couldn't face. In his most morbid moment of acceptance Jake found sudden, instant clarity. He figured it out. There couldn't be that many pieces left. It was Ally. It had always been Ally. It was not by coincidence. Evelyn had been merely a bonus. Emma by the adoption. His vessel. Sebastian in the aftermath of her death. Ally was all that was left of the Morley name. All that was left of his business partner's bloodline. It hadn't ever been a game. It was an agenda.

The duty nurse came in to check her vitals. She told him visiting hours were over. He was quiet. He was polite. "You are gonna have to call security then." She looked down at her patient. She had seen a lot in her twenty odd years of her profession but this lady she thought was something different. She was amazed she was still holding on. "I will let them know you have been authorized to stay until you decide it's time to go." "Goodnight Mr. Madden."

A whisper "Jake?" She scared him. He never could tell. "I'm here." "Talk to me." He eased himself taking great care not to hurt her onto the edge of the bed and cradled her. "I love you Ally." He told her of Shamus and how much her dog missed her. He told her of the Extravaganza describing every detail so she could picture it with her closed eyes. He told her of Tim. He told her of the time when he was twelve his friend had dared him to climb to the very top of a tree and how when he was coming down he fell and broke his arm. She had been sleeping for at least a half hour but it didn't matter. He didn't want to let go of her yet. Her breathing was steady and even. She was okay. Please let her get her through another night.

Could ghosts exact revenge? He thought of Father James. If you do not believe no one will ever change that. God. Demons. Good. Evil. Angels. Spirits. Prayer. Exorcisms. Could a demonic spirit know someone was coming before they were even born? He was abhorred by that. It was blasphemy to even think it. Did this mean that Ally would have ended up like this anyhow? She was always supposed to come to Edgerton? Whether one believed or not Jake thought we are all going to end up in either place. We have our protectors. PROTECTORS. Shamus. Himself. They were the only things that stood in his way. Another piece moved closer to the others. Without them his playground had been opened wide.

The day shift came on. It was six am. Ally was assisted to the rest room. Given liquid nourishment which he coaxed her to at least try. She vomited. Nothing was staying down. Once back in bed and made comfortable Jake asked her if she wanted him to go. She shook her head. "Don't leave me." The charge nurse took that in as she gave her more medication to combat the nausea. "I'm going to send in some warm ginger soda. See if you can get her to drink it." Jake nodded. She was awake. She was here. He found new hope in that. There it was again. Gnawing at him. What was it? He had gone over every word. Over every entry. The dates. He had formed wrong conclusions in that. The dates?

"I'm cold Jake." They brought in a heated blanket. He held her hand. He got her to take a few small sips of the soda. He would try broth at lunch. They brought in her medications. He wondered how often and how large her does were. "She needs these," he was told. "She has episodes without them. Her anxiety never lessens." Ally looked at him. She looked...guilty. She looked ashamed. He couldn't bear that. She had not done this. When the nurse left he told her that. "You are amazing Ally." A tiny smile. Two aides gave her a shower. Another changed the bedding and heated blankets. He brushed her hair. A few more sips of the broth. More hope. Her energy tapped, she slept again.

The dates. That was it. Not the journal dates he had compared. Only one piece left. It had to be. The fire. His earthly death. That date. That was his portal to be reborn. With Ally gone it was the completion of the real cycle. He was one hundred percent sell the farm and bet it all on the horses positive. That was his end game. What had Ally read.

What information had there been? Think damn it. A small voice "Microfiche." For the first time he was overjoyed that she had heard. He had to get to the library. November 5th 1928. Tomorrow. "Tomorrow you son of a Godless whore. Tomorrow you will go away empty handed. You will not take her!"

Before Ally faded off he kissed her lightly. "I love you." "I will be here in the morning and by tomorrow night this will all be over." Her eyes begged for that to be true. He drove back to the Strideway. He was armed with everything he now knew. He would not leave her side. The portal would close hopefully forever. He still was unsure if it would help Ally, she was so far gone in mind and body but if she made it through the cycle would be ruptured. He had to believe that his power would rupture along with it.

At eleven thirty his cell went off. "He's gone Jake. I can't find him anywhere." "I had let him out for the last time and he began to howl so I went to see what was bothering him. He went right through the gate." Jake was up and dressed in two minutes. This was not like him. Shamus had never run off. Never been out of earshot. He pulled up to Josie's and jumped out. The back picket gate was hanging on one hinge. The slats broken and strewn about.

What had gotten into him? Was it both of them being gone? He drove past his house thinking he had to have gone there to wait for him. Nothing. He called out. If Shamus had been in the vicinity he would have come running. Where was he?

His cell went off again for the second time. "Mr. Madden, she's missing!" His heart skipped. "What do you mean she's missing?" His voice urgent. Demanding. "We had a situation. It must have been then." This could not be possible. She wasn't well enough to go anywhere much less on foot in the dark. Sheer panic. Was she lying in a ditch or a field somewhere? "When was this?" "We just noticed. I'm sorry I'm really not sure." He checked his watch. Twelve twenty. Oh God NO! Ally! It was tomorrow. The river. Oh God please no.

He slammed on the brakes and threw the truck into park with the headlight beams still on. He was at a dead run and had to stop fast at the edge of the trestle or he would have gone over. Stones and pebbles broke loose and were cascading down as he skidded to a halt. He was terrified to look in fear that he would see her face down like Emma. "ALLY!" She wasn't there. Please Ally where are you? He opened his arms to the sky and shouted. "PLEASE!" His hands were shaking, where was she? Would he find her in time? It was frigid out here. She had no shoes, no coat. He couldn't have made it this far. That is why she wasn't here. Her body had given out. Where? Where? On the highway Jake sped exceeding all limits heading towards the medical center. As he passed the road to the manor his eye caught the glow of orange over the tree tops.

The fireplace. That was it! That was his portal to take control and claim her. ALLY! He swung the truck around his brakes screeching leaving tread marks in his wake. He saw her through the window. Her gown twisted and filthy. Her feet bleeding. Her hair a matted mess laying crumpled on the great room floor. The sound of the rumbling roar of the glowing chimney was getting louder by the second. He ran to the double doors, kicking them in when out of nowhere Shamus flew by him hurling his 170 pound body through the plate glass sending shards of it flying everywhere. The rumbling was now a deafening roar as the doors gave way. The Rottweiler's powerful jaws were snapping viciously as he lunged into the air with unheard of force. Jake saw him. In that instant he saw the face Ally had described. He could smell its putrid breath. He felt the crash as Shamus connected with it throwing it backwards into the hearth. The fireplace exploded as he dove to cover Ally. The flames were shooting out just above his head cinging his hair and arms before catching the ceiling and beams. He could smell his flesh burning. The searing pain washing over him as he rolled them both out of the way. The stones pelted him. Shattered windows. They slammed into walls. He had to get her out of there. He picked up her lifeless body and screamed for Shamus as he heard the familiar wail of the sirens approaching. The great room was engulfed. He ran to the back of the house and was met by a team of firefighters as they plunged through the side entrance. There just beyond them lay his dog.

He handed off Ally to the EMS attendants who put her on the stretcher and began hastily inserting IVs into her still unconscious frame. Another tech came to him to address his wounds but Jake ran past him and knelt by the dog. He was breathing. He had suffered burns. He was bleeding from the mouth and ears but he was alive. He began to whimper. "Its okay boy," Jake softly crooned. "You did it." "You saved her." The dog seemed to understand. He tried to stand but couldn't. Jake scooped him up and put him in the cab and then he went to the ambulance as they were closing the doors. He was afraid to ask. Afraid to hope. "I don't know. I'm sorry" was his answer. He looked back at the flames coming through the roof on his way to his truck. "Puzzle complete bitch," he ground out tersely, "You lose."

Mike met him at the veterinarian's office. In a small town where everyone knew everyone he had not cared he was ousted from his bed. "We will take good care of him." "Mike can you..." "Go." More records were broken as he pulled into the lot in half the normal drive time. He ran through the Emergency doors. He saw her as he rounded the corner. Still. Ashen. "Please no." Dr. Rainz stepped out of the cubicle. He put his arm on Jake's shoulder. "I'm sorry. I don't know. It's out of our hands now."

He was forced to have his burns cleaned and dressed. Ally. Shamus. His heart was breaking. He was going to be without his world. There were no winners here. Josie showed up just he stepped out to take Mike's call. "He's going to make it Jake. He has a severe concussion. Whatever he hit was massive but he's going to be better than okay in a few weeks." Shamus. He knew. That damn dog knew. That was why he was howling. He sensed her. Why he broke down the gate. The dog had been a blur as passed him going like a freight train doing ninety through that window to the threat on his master. He had taken on the beast and beaten him.

They drank coffee in the lounge as they waited to be able to see her. "I can't lose her Josie." Would she be able to come back from this? How had she been able to get ten steps let alone almost two miles? Would her heart give out? Would her body shut down? If she survived would her mind be gone?" That was death in itself. Unheeded tears. "Please don't take her." It was a quarter past seven am. The sun was just coming up through the waiting room windows. Snow was beginning to fall. "She is asking for you."

The monitors bleeped slowly. Steadily. It was eerily quiet except for that. Her eyes were closed. She had IVs in both arms. Her tiny body wrapped in warmers. Her pallor telling a distinct story. She was dying. She opened her eyes. He had never heard a whisper be almost silent. "Jake?" "I'm afraid." He took her hand and began to cry. "You don't ever have to be afraid again." Her soul was safe. Her place was chosen. They turned down the lights and left them. He cradled her one more time and softly talked to her of the life they were going to have. His tears flowing soundlessly. He told her of all the things that they would do. Of the children and grandchildren they would have.   He talked to her about how when they were old they would have those rockers on the porch like she had seen in magazines.   He talked to her of small towns and a farm with lots of animals.   He talked to her about anything he could think of until he too closed his eyes.   He would stay right here with her. His beautiful Ally.   Silently he cried.

EPILOGUE

It was dark. He could feel her heart beating next to his. He could feel her breathing. He could hear her small voice. "Jake?" She was still here. He took her hand in his he gave up a prayer. "Thank you." It would never be anything less than a miracle. She had been given another chance. Good had overcome the evil that had held her for so long.

Four days later they began to wean her off of the medications. She was eating on her own. Not much but it would take some time for that. She was still fragile but that too would dissipate as she got stronger. She had no recall of walking, of leaving the center. She had no recall of anything from that night. That was a blessing in itself. There was no fear. There was no George Henry. She would never again be the Ally he had met in the restaurant five short months ago neither would he ever be the man he once was. No one gets through an ordeal like this and not wear the scars. None of that mattered. They made it.

At Ally's request Jake brought in a crew and a dozer and leveled what remained of the manor. The insurance adjuster inquired as to a claim. He was told there would not be one. "It is tainted ground. I want nothing from it." "I will never set foot there again."

He and Mike worked tirelessly until there was nothing left but rubble. What had started out as a renovation had forever altered him and the way he would see things. As they turned to go he sent up a prayer for the county who had accepted her gift of the land to them. He spat on the charred overturned ground and its piles of rocks. "Burn in hell."

Made in the USA
Middletown, DE
01 April 2019